A Spell Is Cast

A SPELL
IS CAST

by ELEANOR CAMERON

Illustrated by Beth and Joe Krush

An Atlantic Monthly Press Book

LITTLE, BROWN and COMPANY

Boston · Toronto

ATLANTIC–LITTLE, BROWN BOOKS
ARE PUBLISHED BY
LITTLE, BROWN AND COMPANY
IN ASSOCIATION WITH
THE ATLANTIC MONTHLY PRESS

Published simultaneously in Canada
by Little, Brown & Company (Canada) Limited

PRINTED IN THE UNITED STATES OF AMERICA

For my dear friends, Willie and Agnes, and
for my husband, Ian — you three Scots who,
by being yourselves, have given me so much
for this book.

A Spell Is Cast

One

CORY had fastened her seatbelt with cold fingers when suddenly the airplane tilted, curved right around on one wing so that everyone was sitting on a slant. Out there, level with her eyes, she caught sight of a little yellow plane with a white tail that swooped sideways from them at terrific speed and vanished in purplish-black clouds. Far off stretched a brilliant azure streak behind dark mountains, but here above the plane and all around it, a storm gathered. Broken folds of canyons swung in beneath them, and green velvet squares and furred ridges stretching away to the sea, all crouched under a steely light cast down from the thunderous sky.

The plane sped above the landing strip, touched, bounced, taxied round — and there was the terminal with its metal fence and crowd of people. Everyone unfastened his seatbelt, got up, pulled down coats and bags, and patiently filed out.

"Your uncle will be here to meet you, Cory?" The stewardess leaned over and touched her shoulder.

"Oh, yes — he *said* he would — I think I see —"

"Well, if by any chance there's some mix —"

But she was already pulling away. She was on the ground, running, searching the crowd with darting, hungry eyes for a tall man with a serious face. Grave, almost stern, was the way he had looked in the snapshot he'd sent, not at all like the man she had felt he would be from those letters he had written her, three last year and two this, not counting the note with the snapshot in it. But they were one and the same person, and she knew what would happen. The instant he spied her he would come striding over, smiling, his hand out — "*Hel*-lo, Cory — I'm Uncle Dirk," and he would lean down and give her a hug with one arm and then a quick kiss. She had acted it all out in her mind while the plane rested on the air, moving steadily forward over farms for ants and blue ribbon roads and cliffs and curves of green sea, lurching occasionally or bucking abruptly so that the woman in front of Cory had squealed without dignity, then giggled with a sort of sob, and her husband had hushed her.

Not that man, nor that one — no, nor that one either — too fat. There, *that* one, maybe — the kind-

4

looking one. But he stepped forward and caught up a little boy and tossed him into the air, and he put his arm around the boy's mother and they walked away together, the three of them. And they were all talking at once as fast as they could, with the boy hopping up and down, yanking on his father's arm, and the mother laughing.

Cory stood at the entrance gate with her new red purse and her new gray train case and watched the separate parts of families and couples coming together and going off, while her hands grew colder and her heart heavier until she was left alone.

Never once had it come into her head that Uncle Dirk wouldn't be there. Perhaps Andrew Ferguson, the gardener-chauffeur-handyman, was hunting for her: a clean, wrinkled man, she pictured him, with a brown face and old but respectable clothes. "Miss Cory Winterslow, waiting for Mr. Dirk Van Heusen and bound for Tarnhelm, by any chance?" "Yes, that's me —" But no such person came over.

There was nothing to do but go inside and sit down. Her eyes were dark, almost too large for her face, and soon they knew the whole waiting room by heart, especially the clock on the wall with a long minute hand that jerked forward and stopped, jerked forward and stopped. Then an old lady in a pot-shaped hat all covered with dusty flowers leaned over and asked if someone wasn't coming for her. "Oh, yes," said Cory, just as if she believed it, "my uncle is coming." But after a while the minute hand said that half an hour had passed.

Cory got up and went to the glass doors at the back of the waiting room, as much to get away from the almost unwavering gaze of the old lady as to see if perhaps Uncle Dirk might not be driving up. But he wasn't. Flights kept being announced, and people were paged, but she was not. "Miss Cory Winterslow — paging Miss Cory Winterslow — you're wanted at the desk, please —" But that, of course, was only in her head. The light was becoming sulfurous with a kind of greenish tinge, and the clouds piled behind the hills were getting rounder and blacker and taller. Thunderheads, those were called.

She grasped the silver unicorn hanging on a chain around her neck, then curved the corner of her mouth and tilted her head the way Stephanie, her mother, would do if she were being scornful of something. It was silly for a girl her age to get comfort out of holding a unicorn, even if it *was* an amulet.

"All the same," and she pressed her nose against the cold glass, "I'm worried, and that's the absolute-honesttojiggers truth —"

"What's your name, dearie?"

The words came so suddenly and clearly that Cory

6

jumped, and when she turned, her face flushed red. There was the old woman standing right behind her, too close, and she smiled and blinked at Cory, then nodded toward the desk.

"Why don't you tell me your name, and I'll go ask if anybody left a message for you."

But nobody had.

"Well, then," said the old lady, "the only thing to do is to phone."

Of course! Cory went to the telephone booth and shut herself in, ashamed first of all about not having been called for, and then because it had never occurred to her to do this. She rooted in her purse for a dime and began hunting through the telephone book for Van Heusen. Vacklin, Vagerow, Vajelian (what curious names people have!), Valerian, Valmbalm, Vane, Vaperial, Vaquerious, Varity, Varsity Drugs, Vathland, Vaughan — oh, but Van Heusen would have to come after Vane, wouldn't it? She stared, arranging letters in her head, then ran her finger down the list again, breathing slowly, determined to find it. But it was not there to find. She put the telephone book back in stony despair.

She had dreamed of this, being led from one innocent thing to another until at last she was trapped, not in a place, but in a happening, with no way out. The Van Heusens didn't live at Tarnhelm any more, so they never got the telegram Stephanie had sent telling just when the plane would arrive. That wasn't Uncle Dirk in the snapshot, and whoever was living at Tarnhelm now was playing a trick. Had Stephanie seen the snapshot? No, because Cory had put it right in her purse and Stephanie had been away at the time. She took it out and stared at it, but the man in the picture only stared back with a shadowed gaze that told nothing.

She was "making up," a thing she had done for years, but nevertheless she could have cried. Her hand closed round the unicorn again and she got up and went into the waiting room.

"My family isn't there — in the phone book, I mean."

"And who is your family, dearie?" The old lady watched from under thick, gray brows like a grandfather's, and her eyes were bright and keen and missed nothing, as if, thought Cory, they were determined to ferret out a person's most private affairs.

"The Van Heusens — my uncle and my grandmother."

The old woman's face sharpened. "Ah," she said softly, her eyebrows went right up, and all at once she roused herself. Her black silk coat rustled, her necklaces and chains jangled as she hurried on black pipe-

8

stems to have a look in the directory. The mass of dusty flowers on the pot-shaped hat trembled.

"The Van Heusens!" she exclaimed with relish, then gave a kind of neigh as she searched with her nose through the V's. "*Hah*, would you believe it! Here, give me your dime —" She dialed, asked a question or two, then sniffed and put back the receiver. "Not listed," she said. "Wouldn't you know. Well — no, wait. Your uncle has an office. What's his partner's name? Yes, here it is." She dialed again, and when she had explained to the person on the other end about Cory, there came a quacking, so loud that the old lady had to hold the receiver away. "Well, what about his house, then?" she said finally. "Will you give me the number?" More quacking, and the old woman started to turn as if to ask Cory to put a number down, but then went on listening. "Nobody there either, eh? Well, would you tell Mr. Van Heusen, if he happens to call in, that Mrs. Smallwood telephoned? He'll know my name. We go right by the house, so we'll just take her along and have her there in two ticks. Yes — say the Smallwoods have taken her. That's right. Goodbye." She hung up. "So that's that. Come along, child. His secretary said they weren't expecting to meet anyone s'far as *she* knew. Downright peculiar, I'd say. Your uncle's off on a job way up in the hills somewhere, an' doesn't expect to be home for dinner, was what the secretary gathered from what he'd said. Wonder where your grandma is."

"Well," said Cory, "I'm wondering about Fergie and Andrew — Fergie's Andrew's wife and she's the housekeeper. Maybe they're not going to be there either." She pictured a big, black, utterly deserted house, and her heart felt squeezed.

"Oh, I expect they've just gone off to do the shopping, an' your grandma's out to tea. Don't you worry about *that* —"

"I'm not wor— at least not much," said Cory.

"Here comes Persis." With surprising agility Mrs. Smallwood gathered together a great many parcels and hustled over to the door. "Pers!" she called. "Got a rider. Van Heusens —" She drew up her mouth and lifted her shoulders. "Never came and not a word out of 'em. Now, dearie, don't forget your case."

In came Pers, neat and quick, and began taking some of his wife's bundles.

"That everything, Hattie? Let's get along —"

"But what if —" began Cory, feeling shoved and nudged before she had even had time to think.

"Y'mean, what if your uncle takes a mind to show up after all?" finished Mrs. Smallwood, giving Cory a poke forward. "Serve him right, I'd say." She followed her husband through the door, and Cory found herself trotting along in between.

"But my suitcases! Oh, Mrs. Smallwood, I'd really rather —"

"The child's suitcases, of course," exclaimed the old woman. "Where's your baggage tickets? Here, Pers, run back in and get 'em. And you be sure and tell the man at the desk that the young lady for Tarnhelm is being taken by the Smallwoods." Away went Pers.

"Mrs. Smallwood, my mother told me never to go off with strangers, and that if I —"

"Strangers!" cried Mrs. Smallwood. "Who said anything about strangers?" She gave a sudden chuckle and her shrewd little eyes held something gay and mocking in their depths.

"My mother said I never should
Play with the gypsies in the wood —"

she piped in a tuneless treble. "Here's Pers a'ready. My, *that* was speedy!"

While the boxes and bags were being stowed away in an old, black, shiny sedan that sat high on its wheels like a dowager in too short skirts, a drop of rain plopped on Cory's cheek and the wind rushed at them in a chill, fierce flurry.

"Downpour, all right," observed Mr. Smallwood, wrinkling up his face and staring at the sky. "Real gully-washer. Hop in, little lady —" But she shouldn't! She shouldn't! Yet as if in a dream, whether she wanted to or not, she got in. "You just sit right there in the back, and we'll have you along in no time."

As they swerved out of the airport, Mr. Smallwood maneuvering grandly, and drove along toward Monterey, the rain started to pelt.

"Where'd you say you was from, dearie?" demanded Mrs. Smallwood, screwing her head partway round.

"New York — on the jet," said Cory proudly.

"*Alone?*" cried Mrs. Smallwood. "All the way from back East?"

"Oh, yes. I'm old enough. It wasn't bumpy like the little plane — it was mag-*nif*-icent — though I could see lots more from the prop-jet. A friend of my mother's met me at the San Francisco airport and treated me to lunch, and then made sure I got on."

"Yes, I know," said Mrs. Smallwood. "I saw you, but I had to sit clear in the back — I'd been visiting my daughter. So that's called a prop-jet."

"A propeller-jet. But it isn't *anything* like a real jet. Not even slightly."

Mrs. Smallwood seemed to take this in, then began murmuring to Persis, and she sounded, thought Cory, exactly like a teakettle simmering. Sometimes her murmurs lowered to whispering full of vigorous *s*'s, and the flowers on her hat bobbed, and Persis said, "Hmmmph — mmm-hmph —" But anybody knows it's impolite to whisper in front of people. It makes the third person feel as if he isn't wanted or is in the way, as if the whispering must be about him. What were they planning? What was there to whisper about her?

I think, said Cory to herself, making up again, that Mrs. Smallwood is a witch and she's persuading Mr. Smallwood that they should put an enchantment on me. But I have a feeling she has already, beginning with my not finding Van Heusen in the phone book. Mr. Smallwood doesn't look a bit like a witch's husband, but that's exactly why Mrs. Smallwood chose him, and they're going to keep me to sweep the hearth and milk the cow and gather fagots and catch the neighbors' chickens for dinner and steal eggs for breakfast, and nobody'll ever know what's happened to me, because Mr. Smallwood didn't really give my name to the man at the desk, and I'll just disappear and never be allowed to grow up. "— the young lady for Tarnhelm is being taken by the Smallwoods."

Cory's hand went up to the silver unicorn and she stared out of the window through the rain at green hills covered with dark clumps of oaks under which, in some fields, cattle clustered.

Now here they were in a town, which must be Monterey, then they were spinning along a curving road bordered thickly on either hand with tall pines misted over with rain. On and on they went, and sometimes, to the right, Cory would catch vague, far-off glimpses of the sea, then into the pines they went again until on the left she saw, set some distance back, a large, white, rambling building with a tall tower that Mr. Smallwood said was the Carmelite Monastery. And he said he sometimes thought of the nuns in there, working and reading and praying and contemplating and now and then, perhaps, looking out over the sea. "A monastery for *nuns?*" asked Cory. But a monastery was for either monks or nuns, said Mr. Smallwood, and Mrs. Smallwood said she'd seen them going for walks on the sand with their veils blowing. Those were sisters from the neighboring Notre Dame retreat, Mr. Smallwood told her. Across from the monastery stretched a wide beach with the gray waves pounding over in long frothing rollers, and a little farther on was the thick forest again.

"Right here," said Mr. Smallwood, "I saw a mallard duck and his family going along by the side of the road, him in front with his green head, and all the rest following in a line."

"You never did!" said Mrs. Smallwood.

"Oh, yes I did so," said Mr. Smallwood.

14

Now came a dark, curving point of wooded land reaching out into the ocean, and at the entrance was a big sign made out of cut logs that said, Cory read quickly: POINT LOBOS RESERVE.

"Uncle Dirk's going to take me!" she burst out, her spirits leaping and a spurt of excitement coming back. Surely they must be headed in the direction of Tarnhelm and surely everything was going to turn out all right after all. "He said he would, and if he said it I know he will. He wrote in his letter that Fergie — that's Andrew Ferguson's wife — will make us a picnic lunch, and he'll take me to the sea lion rocks, and the bird island where the cormorants and the gulls and the pelicans are. Do you know my uncle, Mrs. Smallwood?"

Mrs. Smallwood seemed not to hear. But then:

"That young gentleman," she said finally, in a tight, pursed up voice, "never has so much as a smile for anybody. I've never had one out of him in my whole life."

Cory was silent, seeing the man in the snapshot.

"And my grandmother?"

"Yes, your grandma. She's society, always going out to teas and lunches — luncheons, they call 'em — and dinners and all like that. Symphonies and the drama, and *that's* not picture shows. I meet her on the street and she notices me if she feels like it, and doesn't if

15

she doesn't. She looks through a person as if he wasn't there, but don't tell me she doesn't see, because *I* know she does —"

"Now, Hattie —" said Mr. Smallwood. "What's the little —"

"Well, I don't care, it's the truth. I only say what's true —"

Mrs. Smallwood's voice trembled, and Cory remembered that no matter how many questions she had asked Stephanie about Grandmother Van Heusen, Stephanie slid away from them like a cat sliding out from under your hand.

Suddenly Mrs. Smallwood leaned forward.

"Look there!" she cried. "Stop, Pers — stop, I say. It's that Hawthorne boy — what's-his-name — my sakes, he'll be soaked to the skin!"

Mr. Smallwood honked and slowed and drew to the side of the road, Mrs. Smallwood knocked briskly on the window, and almost before Cory could blink the door was wrenched open and into the back leaped a wet, wind-whipped, ocean-smelling, vigorous, grinning boy.

"Hi! W*ow*, what luck —" and he would have flopped down right on top of Cory if she hadn't nipped over in the nick of time. "Am I ever absolutely *sopped!*" He turned his round freckled face and beamed triumphantly at her as if the very height of

success was to be as dripping as he was. His thick, red-dish-brown hair was plastered to his head.

Cory folded up her legs and moved away along the old, rubbed upholstery that smelled of dog. Now the mixture of the boy's wet sweater and the doggy smell of the seats was quite strong.

"Look — it's letting up!" he shouted. "By golly, if that isn't just like rain. You're walking home and it comes down in buckets. You get a ride and it stops.

What's your name?" He turned and looked at her as
if he really wanted to know and wasn't just asking to
be saying something. The instant she told him, he
said, "Mine's Peter Hawthorne," and they solemnly
shook hands. "On account of me being president of
the Explorers Club, I was exploring after school.
And on account of living the farthest out of anyone,
I've got a long way to get back home."

Peter filled the car with his liveliness and vigor and
enthusiasm. He himself was a gust of the rainy, pun-
gent-smelling wind, so that even if his sweater smelled
and he was getting her rather damp on one side, Cory
didn't care. She liked his grin and his freckles and his
sea-green eyes and the way he'd asked her what her
name was.

"Do you live near a big house called Tarnhelm?"

"Tarnhelm! You're going *there?*" He looked appalled. "To *stay?*" he added, taking in the suitcase on
the floor and the other on the seat beside her with the
train case on it. "Wheeeee-ee-ew —" His long-drawn-
out whistle fell away like a fading-out firework. "I'll be
darned."

"But why not?" Cory wanted to know, anxious all
over again. "That's where my uncle and grandmother
live."

"They do? The Van Heusens? I used to play Tarnhelm was a castle when I was a kid," said Peter, as if

he were a hundred, "because it's so big and all built of stone. It sticks up out of the trees on the next point from our house and frowns out over the sea. We live on one point, then there's a gorge in between with cliffs and pines and things, then another jutting-out point where Tarnhelm is. How did it get that name? It's like you'd find in *Kidnapped* —"

This was what Cory had always thought.

"My mother gave it that name when she was my age — she must have made it up, or maybe she found it in a book. She can't remember. But she always called it that, and then everybody else began to, and Grandmother had it put on her stationery and Uncle Dirk wrote me that he made a big sign when he was about fifteen or sixteen and put it up, and he said it's been there ever since."

"Yes," said Peter. "A big board with a unicorn carved on it."

Cory stared at him.

"A unicorn!" Her eyes met his, startled. "It must be magic."

Peter didn't laugh at her.

"How do you know?"

"Look!" She held out her own unicorn on the chain around her neck. Smaller than the top joint of her thumb, it was, with every line of the mane and tail, the hoofs, nostrils, eyes and ears and long single horn, forward-tilting and narrowing straight to a point, etched clear and clean. One front hoof was held higher than the other as though the unicorn were leaping, rampant.

"I'll bet it's a family crest," said Peter.

"But Stephanie never said it was, and she would have told me. I've had this unicorn as long as I can remember. It's my amulet. Anyway, if Uncle Dirk likes unicorns, he'll be all right and I'll like *him*."

"So you're afraid you won't," said Peter.

"Well, now," said Mrs. Smallwood, "here you are, my boy. Lucky we hap —"

And no sooner had she turned her head than the dowager coughed and hiccoughed, coughed and stopped, went on for a bit and stopped dead. Mrs. Smallwood stiffened and was still for a moment.

"Persis, *you — don't — mean to tell me — that for the third time this year you've —*"

"Now, now, Hattie, don't go and get all fired up! We'll just have Peter give us a shove and we'll coast right down the hill — it's only just ahead there. Then it won't take me but about fifteen minutes or so to walk to the gas station —"

"Fifteen minutes!" cried his wife, outraged. "While I sit there twiddling my thumbs! Oh, I could just — and that's clear on beyond where this child has to go, not to speak of the long way up to the house from the road —"

"But that's all right, Mrs. Smallwood," interrupted Peter eagerly. "She can get out here with me and I'll take her to Tarnhelm. It isn't far — I know the way. Being an Explorer, I know every road and trail around here."

Cory had begun to feel anxious and uncertain again. What if Uncle Dirk had gone to the airport and then got home, and she didn't come and she didn't come, waiting for Mr. Smallwood to go for the gas and walk all the way back to the car? But now she was filled, at Peter's words, with calm confidence, and Mr. Smallwood seemed enormously relieved.

"Good!" he exclaimed. "Good! Now get her bag, Peter — no reason you can't take one of 'em along, and we'll come by with the other tomorrow morning. When you get out, both you young ones can give us a shove."

A moment or so later the dowager was rolling away down the grade through the pines, and Peter and Cory, watching her, were left standing on the highway with Cory's suitcase.

"*This* isn't very heavy," said Peter, hefting it. "The way you talked, I thought it'd weigh a ton."

Cory picked up her train case and slid the strap of

her purse over her arm. She looked up at the black sky that seemed to press lower and lower, and there came a mutter of thunder like a dog growling in its throat.

"Peter," she said, "what if it starts raining again? Shouldn't we go to your house first?"

"Nope, because mine's about as far from here as Tarnhelm is. Come on, I'll show you a shortcut."

Two

THE ROAD that curved away ahead and behind was deserted. Now all was silent — no, not quite silent, for Cory caught the muffled voice of the sea, and high overhead the wind in the pines mingled with the ocean's rough breathing — *h-a-ahh, u-hh-ha-aaa-aah,* as if a giant were asleep in there among the trees. Not a house was in sight, not even a woodman's cottage, observed Cory, only the dark forest where a narrow trail began at the highway's edge with a sign that said: THE HAWTHORNES.

"But I thought that *you* said it wouldn't be any closer to go to your house than right to Tarnhelm."

"Well, it wouldn't — *much,* because of the short-cut," said Peter hastily, starting off at once along the trail. "There's a road farther along in here that leads to our house, and the Van Heusens use it too, and when it gets to their property, that's where the big sign is with the unicorn on it. But it's ages and *ages* up to their place after you get past the sign."

"Is the shortcut easy?"

"Not very. But of course it isn't anything for an Explorer."

They walked on in silence, the suitcase bumping and bumping against Peter's legs, and pretty soon he dropped it, heaved a breath, and took it up again.

"It *is* heavy, isn't it, Peter? I told you it was —"

"Not for me, it isn't. Explorers have to do all sorts of hard things and this is nothing. You wait and see —"

"You mean I could be an Explorer too?" She hurried so that she came alongside of him and could watch his face. "You mean you'd take me in?"

"But *I* couldn't," laughed Peter. "You've got to be voted in. Look, here's the road and that's the sign and up there's the castle." He put down her suitcase and pointed ahead to where a gray stone shape rose out of the trees that covered the headland.

Cory took in the thick wooden slab, weathered to silvery gray, that hung from a black metal standard at the side of the drive, and studied with wondering eyes the unicorn carved deeply into it and painted white, as were the words *Tarnhelm* and *The Van Heusens*. This unicorn, exactly like her own, stood on its hind legs with its forefeet rampant and its neck curved. Then she looked beyond to the big stone house.

"First I meet Mrs. Smallwood, and then — what does your father do, Peter — I mean for a living?"

"He's in the lumbering business."

"Yes, it all fits in. First I meet Mrs. Smallwood, then the woodcutter's son, and now there's the castle," she said under her breath, "where the Wicked Queen lives, and the Black Prince —"

"That's a good name for him," said Peter. "He's got black hair and black eyebrows, and he's mean — well, stern, anyhow. When I found a dug-in place under some rocks on the side of their property up over the sea, he yelled at me to go away and he was mad as hops."

Cory set her mouth in a way she had when she was determined not to believe something. She would have bet anything Uncle Dirk wasn't like what Peter said. Besides, he'd carved that unicorn up there.

Here at the entrance to Tarnhelm property, the road divided, one branch going up to the stone house on the left and the other off to the Hawthornes' on the right. Now Peter led her away from the road, straight out toward the sea, and when they came to the edge of the bluff, still among trees, Cory looked over into a gorge filled with enormous boulders and with pines growing up thickly, and the waves curled over and rolled in along a little beach at the mouth of the gorge.

Then they went along the edge into the open. Cory had her head down, but lifted it all at once and was faced with the whole tremendous sweep of the Pacific. Back in New York she had seen the Atlantic from among a mass of people at Coney Island on glaring afternoons smelling of hot dogs and mustard and pickles and suntan oil, but never anything like this. Vast and wild, the sea plunged in under a strange purplish-green sky. White gulls were tossed on invisible arcs of air — skimming, soaring, calling. And she saw the lonely headlands, one after another as far as her sight could reach, breasting the incoming rollers like the prows of huge ships, and the waves crashing at their feet in bursts of foam. She drew in a stinging breath of wind and felt as if she could have shouted, "Peter — Peter — I can look out over this every day — *every single day!*"

But she did not shout. She kept her joy pressed back, and silently followed him across a broad terrace covered with low-growing shrubs and short, tough grass scattered with orange and yellow and pink and cream-colored flowers.

"Back there, on the other side of my house," said Peter, gesturing widely, "at the bottom of a whole lot of wooden steps, there's a big long beach and beyond that are the bird rocks and Point Lobos."

Cory turned to look.

"Uncle Dirk and I are going there, maybe tomorrow. He promised me — he wrote me all about it."

"Well, I'll bet you don't go. I'll bet anything. You mean he's written you a real letter, or just a little scrabbly note like I get from my relatives?"

"A real letter. The Christmas before last I wrote him and Grandmother to say thank you for my Christmas gifts, and I guess I told them a lot because about two months after that Uncle Dirk wrote back, a simply stu-*pen*dous letter. I don't mean long but the best letter anybody ever wrote me, all about the country around here, and how it was when he was a boy, and what he used to do, and it was funny in places —"

"*Funny!*" burst out Peter, completely astonished.

"— and so then I answered, and we've written ever since."

Now the meadow-like terrace was narrowing and the going became so difficult that Cory could not imagine how Peter managed to hang on to her suitcase. Yet what was there to do with it? If he had put it down, it would have slid right away out of sight. As for her smaller case, she knew that after a while, when the trail became much steeper and rougher, she was going to have to leave it, and what would her grand-mother say? Her heart beat painfully. Even though she could see that this path must cut off a great deal of the winding road that led by degrees up to the stone house, it was too hard — much, much too hard to follow.

"Peter —" she began, and stood there trembling with one hand clutched around the handle of her case and her purse pressed against it so that she could keep the other hand free to catch at bushes and holding-on places in the rocks. "Peter —" Then she stopped, because if she had said what she felt like say-ing he would never have let her in to the Explorers. Instead, she turned, shaken to the pit of her stomach, and stared out over the sea.

For there had come a sharp crackle together with a hurting flash that lit up the entire heavens, and Cory saw a dark, wavering curtain sweeping toward them over the flattened water — a living thing that glided swiftly forward on invisible feet.

"That's *it!*" shouted Peter. "The storm! Come on, Cory — we'll be —" but the rest of his words were swallowed in a crash that shook the cliffs and bellowed away and away, the echoes tunneling like cannon shots across the water. On came the black curtain, a kind of dense, moving veil that in a moment would engulf them. Cory stared at it in terror, and again the lightning flashed and crackled, and she looked up ahead and there was Peter waving at her to hurry — hurry —

"The cave!" he yelled.

Up she went, stumbling, banging her shins until they bled, and no sooner did the storm reach them than Peter grabbed her by the arm and hauled her in under the rocks. She crouched down gasping for breath, wondering if her chest were going to burst. Then she raised up and looked around. It was very dim in here, but she could see her suitcase wedged in behind Peter, and what with that and her smaller case and the two of them, there was just room, if they stayed curled up, to keep sheltered and dry. Across the mouth of the cave, which did not directly face the sea, drove a solid sheet of rain, and it made a tremendous lashing, pouring sound as if it would never stop.

"Isn't this neat?" shouted Peter. "Did you ever see such a neat place in your life?"

Solemnly Cory nodded and crouched back a little farther when a sudden shift of wind sent a gust of rain in at them.

"It's cozy!" she shouted back. She pulled her skirt down over her knees and locked her arms around her legs. All at once she felt pleased. There was just enough space between them and the mouth of the cave, a margin of a few feet, so that the gusts couldn't quite reach them under the overhang of rocks above the entrance. It was like a little house, a little snug house — this "dug-in place," Peter had called it — and they'd reached it just in the nick of time. They were protected and safe as badgers in a burrow.

She saw Peter grinning at her, then he put back his head and laughed aloud, a short, sharp laugh of triumph, and she knew that his eyes, his very freckles, his blunt nose and wide happy mouth would all be triumphant.

In a little while the rain slackened and suddenly Cory thought of something.

"Peter, what if Uncle Dirk's secretary was wrong, and he and Grandmother are wondering where I am?"

"Well, they'll just have to wonder," said Peter sensibly, "because what can we do?"

"But what about your folks? Won't your mother be wondering what's happened to you all this time, out in the storm? My mother would be simply frantic."

"I'll bet that's what *she* says — '*sim*ply frantic'!" mimicked Peter, and his eyebrows rose into semicircles and he shrugged up his shoulders and closed his eyes. He was making fun of her, but he looked so comical she couldn't help laughing.

30

"That's exactly what Stephanie says, and that's just exactly what she does —"

"Who's Stephanie?"

"Why, my mother. I *told* you —"

"You mean you call her by her first name? That's the weirdest thing I ever heard of. I can imagine what would happen if I tried calling my mother Sally. She'd wallop me. It sounds as if she's your sister or something."

"Well, she's my mother. That is, I'm adopted, so maybe that's why she likes me to call her Stephanie. She's an actress, but a special kind called a monologist."

"A m'*nol*ugist! What's that? I never heard of anyone called by that name. What does she do — tell fortunes or something? Is she some kind of crystal-gazer?"

"No!" said Cory indignantly. "That means she's an actress who makes up her own plays and songs and puts on a whole show all by herself, with someone to play the piano when she sings. And you should see her dresses — all kinds, and *beau*-tiful! For about an hour and a half, with a ten-minute intermission in the middle, she does different skits, being any sort of person you can think of — a young girl, or an old woman, or someone from Brooklyn or Mexico or Hollywood or France. Or she can be a cockney or a noble British lady, or Irish or Scotch or — just anything. The best fun is when she's working on a new one and I can be the audience. You should just see her work — I don't know how she does it! And she memorizes like lightning. When she's on tour she travels all over."

"And you go with her?"asked Peter in awe.

Cory was silent. She picked up a stick and began scratching designs on the floor of the cave.

"No," she said after a little. "I have to stay home because of school."

"But there're summer vacations," persisted Peter. "Do you mean you stay home all *alone?* Don't you have a father?"

"No, I don't. Stephanie hasn't got a husband — she's Miss Van Heusen. And we always have lady-helps, but mostly they're no good. I mean they don't want to talk, and when I make up stories they're too busy to listen or they want to read their old magazines and all they say is, 'Now, that'll do, Cory,' or 'Hadn't you better go straighten up your room?' or 'I *never* — what a chatterbox you are — you mustn't tell such fibs.' The only lady-help we ever had who could imagine better than I can was quite young and her name was Maureen McQueeny and she stayed three months and it was heaven. Then she got married. I was horribly disappointed but not at all surprised."

32

"But you make friends at school, don't you?"

"A few," evaded Cory, not wanting to admit how few, because it's hard when you have to start all over again every so often. "We move around a lot, so I'm always going to new schools."

"How many?"

"Well, let me see — five. The first was a private school and I loved it, but then Stephanie bought a big house out in the country that cost too much money, so she couldn't afford that school and I went to another. But I was awfully unhappy there so she sent me to a third one. Then she had to sell the house and we moved into an apartment in New York and I went to a public school. But just as I was getting to know some of the kids, we moved out of that apartment to the one where we are now, so I had to change again."

"Oh," said Peter. "Well, I'd hate that. It's too bad you can't stay here and go to my school."

Cory looked up from her design-making and studied him.

"Do you suppose I could, Peter?" For a moment she was filled with hope. "I never thought of that. We couldn't seem to get the right lady-help when Stephanie had to go away this time, so because it's Easter vacation, she thought it would be a good chance for me to visit Uncle Dirk and Grandmother.

I've never seen them, you know, and I wanted to because of Stephanie telling me about growing up here, and because of Uncle Dirk writing me about the cliffs and the ocean and the birds and the redwoods at Big Sur. Have you been there?"

"*Loads* of times — the Explorers go hiking all over."

"Peter, do you suppose if I went to your school and the Explorers got to know me, they'd let me join? I've never belonged to a club in my whole life."

"I don't think so," said Peter. "Really, it's just for boys —"

"But you do have some girls?"

"Only two," he answered with definite finality as if they had barely squeaked in and there were to be absolutely no more. "You have to do something special to get in, and you're so kind of thin and pale I don't know what you could do. Then we didn't exactly take in Bip and Maxie. They were just part of the club in the very beginning. They're awfully good at hiking and swimming and climbing cliffs and rocks and trees or whatever there is to go up, and they can swim as well as the boys."

"They can?" said Cory faintly. She couldn't swim a stroke and she hadn't had a chance to do much hiking or climbing, so that was that. And when she thought of all that Mrs. Smallwood had said about Grandmother and about Uncle Dirk, and what Peter had said about him, she felt there wasn't even the faintest hope that they would let her stay and go to Peter's school. Of course, the person who had sent her those letters would let her stay, but not the dark, angry man who had yelled at Peter and told him to get off his property.

"It's so strange," said Cory.

But now Peter was peering out of the cave.

"Look," he said. "It's hardly raining at all. We'd better go because if we stay here any longer it's liable to start pouring again. Come on!" Out he went, then leaned over and stuck his head in. "Just leave everything — your suitcase and that other little bag and your purse. We can get along faster that way."

"But my pajamas!" protested Cory. "What'll I do without my stuff, Peter?"

"Well, tonight won't matter — and I'll come back here tomorrow and bring 'em up."

All the same, Cory took her purse and then scrabbled out of the cave after Peter. It was raining harder again, and for a second she was tempted to say they must get back inside. Yet they could not stay there all night. Was it getting to be night or was this darkness only a more intense storm darkness? At least it must be evening, because there was a certain feeling in the air, a look about the sky that suggested that day was gone. And they were getting soaked — and the bushes they pressed through were so wet that after a little their shoes made a squelching sound — and mine were brand-new, thought Cory, when I left New York.

But the worst was ahead. When they got to the steep wooded slope that they must climb before reaching Tarnhelm itself, Cory kept slipping so that her knees and hands, the front of her coat, her purse, and even her sleeves became covered with mud. It made her furious, and her fury grew and grew until finally she exploded.

"We should *never* have come this way, Peter Hawthorne. No matter *how* long it was to go by the road, we wouldn't have gotten all messed up like this, and I'll bet you *any*thing the only reason we didn't go to your house was because you wanted to stay in the cave during the storm and climb up this hill!"

"There, you see?" shouted Peter, turning and grinning down at her, merry and mocking. "That's why girls like you can't get into the Explorers. They're always fussing about getting messed up. Besides, you don't know anything about that road up there — it's miles and miles and *miles* — and there wouldn't have been any cave, either."

He leaped swiftly on ahead and she knew that there wasn't any use saying one more word. Besides, here they were at the top. She stood there with her face scarlet in spite of the icy rain. She tossed back her wet hair, wiped her hands down the sides of her coat where there wasn't as much mud, then followed Peter over a low stone wall and across an enormous sweep of lawn toward the black shape of Tarnhelm, scattered with winking lights in among oaks and pines and cypresses.

At the sight of those lights, Cory gave a gasp of relief — at least Fergie and Andrew were at home. Or at least *someone* was. But she was aware that her stomach felt peculiar, heavy and kind of sick. What was it? Excitement? Suspense? Or dread, because of her clothes and shoes? What would Grandmother and Uncle Dirk say when they saw her ruined state? Would they be terribly angry? Yet how could they be when they had not even troubled to come to the plane and get her? *Why hadn't they?*

The lawn was like a castle's lawn, it was that vast. Then they came to the trees, whose dripping branches creaked as they rubbed against one another; and Cory and Peter went in under them along a needle-strewn path to the house itself, where a row of windows revealed a bowed head moving back and forth as if the person were working there.

"I bet you that's the kitchen," said Peter, "because this is toward the back of the house."

They raced up onto the covered porch, where big logs were stacked neatly in a pile at one side, with an-

37

other pile of smaller pieces ranged in orderly ranks nearby. Peter began knocking, very loudly, without the slightest timidity or hesitation, but Cory was shaking, and whether it was with cold or fear she did not know.

The next instant the door flew open. And there stood somebody — a woman — with her back to the light so that Cory couldn't make out her face, but then the woman reached out to one side and the porch light went on, and she stood staring at them in horrified, appalled, almost unbelieving astonishment, as if they'd risen from the dead. It was Fergie, Cory knew in an instant, because she was exactly as Cory had imagined her — rather short, rather stout, with a lively, expressive face and pink cheeks, and she had a big, clean, starched apron on.

"*Oh!*" cried Fergie. "Oh, it can't be — it can't —" and her hands went up to her head. Then all at once she stepped forward and took Cory's face and her wet, dark, perfectly straight hair between both palms and kissed her. "My wee spalpeen — what in the wurrrrld could have happened! Mr. Dur-rk's secretary called the minute we got back and said the Smallwoods would be bringing ye, and so I've been waiting and waiting for the car to come, and it didn't, and the Smallwoods aren't home yet, and I've been just sick.

Come in — come in! You, too, Peter — come in at once!"

Cory caught a warm whiff of richness, the richness of roasting meat, of something baking that smelled crusty and buttery, and something pungent that made her mouth water. Then Peter brushed by, Fergie's arm went round her, and the door was closed at last on the cold and sodden world outside.

Three

FOR AN instant, as Fergie took in their wretched-ness — mud, drenched clothing, Cory's scratched and bloody knees — she could not seem to get her wits to-gether.

But half an hour later, there were the two of them washed and clean and dry, Cory wrapped in Fergie's bathrobe and with Fergie's slippers on her feet (they were not much too large), and Peter in Andrew's bathrobe and a pair of Andrew's thick heather-colored wool socks, and both of the children in wicker basket chairs near the stove, where Fergie was putting the last touches on their dinner.

All the time they'd been getting out of their wet things and into the bathrobes, Peter in the kitchen and Cory in Fergie and Andrew's sitting room next to it, Peter had constantly shouted interruptions to what Cory was telling. But nobody minded, and bit by bit the whole story came out, with Fergie making her own exclamations and stopping every now and then to stare in amazement.

"But what I cannot understand is that the telegram from Miss Stephanie said ye would arrive tomorrow!" and then, "Ye *don't* mean to tell me those Smallwoods ran out of gas again — and ye don't mean they left ye to make yer way here all alone and with a stor-rm coming on!" and finally, "Around by the *ocean?* But ye'll never have managed to creep along there! Why, there's not room for a fly — Peter, Peter, ye shouldn't have done it. And ye mean with all that water coming down, ye went and crawled up the side of the hill just below the wall? And yer suitcase, Cory! It's still down there, ye say — and yer train case too? But how in the wurr-rrld are we to —"

"I'll get them, Fergie," said Peter. "Don't worry — the Explorers'll bring them up first thing tomorrow morning, and that's a promise."

Fergie could not get over the telegram. Her blue eyes widened.

"Fur-rst Miss Stephanie wired one thing, and then another, until we were all helter-skelter and had no idea what she meant to do. I don't know how many dates she sent yer granny ye were coming, and yer granny got all wur-rked up. Tchk!"

"And will my grandmother be furious with me, Fergie, do you think — I mean for ruining my shoes and getting sopped and getting my coat all muddy?"

"Well, p'raps it'd be best if we didn't go into all that about the cave and creeping along the cliffs in the rain. I doubt yer granny would understand. Now, Peter, you go phone yer father to come with dry things after a bit. Here comes Andrew, back from picking up some plants at the nur-rsery. He could take ye home, but ye cannot go home in a bathrobe in this weather, and besides, it'd be best for ye both to just sit down and have hot dinners this minute."

"I'll say it would," agreed Peter fervently, watching, with his green eyes growing darker, as Fergie drew from the oven a large, golden-crusted beef pie whose fragrance wafted forth so tantalizingly that Cory could hardly bear it. Peter tore himself away to phone as quickly as possible to tell his dad not to come for a long, *long* time, while at the same moment there was heard a stamping outside the back door. It opened, and here came a voice singing with great vigor:

> *"Hey, Jock-ma-cuddy,*
> *Ma cuddy's o'er the dike —*
> *An' if ye touch ma cuddy,*
> *Ma cuddy'll gie ye a bite — hooch!"*

With that "hooch!"— which sounded almost like "hook-h-h!"— in from the porch stepped a wiry little

43

man not much taller than Fergie, and when he saw Cory, she thought his big bronze eyes would jump right out of his head. Up went his eyebrows, and he pointed and cried out, as if she'd appeared suddenly from under a plate:

"It'll never be the lassie herself — !"

"Aye, it will be," replied Fergie solemnly, putting the beef pie on the table.

"It *is!*" said Cory in huge delight. "Nobody came, so the Smallwoods brought me, and then Peter took me along the cliffs and we stayed in a cave —"

Andrew sank into his chair as if he couldn't take the news standing up, and then Peter came back and they all sat down around the table and Peter and Cory told Andrew everything that had happened while Fergie served dinner, and Cory decided, as Andrew listened, that his eyes were exactly the color of that gleaming golden-brown moss you see on stones under the clear water of running brooks. She'd never known anyone in her life with eyes that color. In fact, she'd never in her life known anyone like Andrew or Fergie, and she felt she was beginning to love them already. Nobody — not Stephanie, and certainly not any lady-help, except Maureen McQueeny — who had ever come to the apartment had listened like this: with their whole hearts and with all sorts of satisfying questions and exclamations of wonder. They made you

45

feel that nobody had ever had such adventures as yours.

Then all at once Fergie said, "All right now, Andrew — grace, please."

And Andrew bent his head and recited:

> *"Some hae meat an' canna eat,*
> *An' some hae nane that want it —*
> *But we hae meat, an' we can eat,*
> *So let the Lord be thankit."*

Then he looked round, lifted his fork and said, "Wire in!" Which they all did. That is, they began. "Look there, now — would ye believe it — the lassie's cawry-fisted!" exclaimed Andrew.

"What's that?" asked Cory, puzzled.

"Why, left-handed. It's Scottish for left-handed," explained Fergie.

"And her *name's* Cory," said Peter. "That's funny."

"P'raps that's why she's Cory," said Andrew. "At any rate, she's bewitched. Did ye not know left-handed people are bewitched, lassie?"

"Not bewitched, Andrew — enchanted," put in Fergie. "Or maybe they're the same thing. Are they, now?"

But nobody was quite sure. And all this time the

beef pie was disappearing, the crust of which was as rich and melting as it had smelled, oozing with brown gravy and covering chunks of tender, succulent beef of such a flavor that Cory had to have two large helpings and Peter three, so that everyone thought he would "bur-r-rst!" as Fergie said. And there were creamed onions and coleslaw and a green salad with thick slices of tomato, and homemade bread with plenty of butter, and also damson plum jam to spread on as thick as you pleased. As for the pungent fragrance that had made Cory's mouth water, it was mince pie, which they had hot with a choice of hard sauce or lemon sauce. And this was because, though it was neither Thanksgiving nor Christmas, Andrew liked mince pie so much that Fergie made it for him every few weeks.

"O-o-oh, *lucky!*" groaned Peter in passionate envy, whereupon Fergie said that the next time she made it, they would call him to come for dinner and he should have all the mince pie he wanted. Cory thought this must be a dream, Peter coming to eat with them, and Fergie making meals like this, and Andrew listening to their talk with his eyes shining. She wondered if she would wake up and find herself in New York again with one of the lady-helps shaking her to get out of bed and get ready for school. They had always gotten meals out of cans and jars and packages and never,

never made anything themselves except Maureen Mc-Queeny, who had loved to cook.

"Ah, well," sighed Andrew at last, "all I can say is, it's a most for-rtunate business yer granny isn't at home just now. Of course, what with the telegram saying ye'd arrive tomorrow, she never thought to stay home — nor Mr. Dur-rk either."

"Of course now, Cory dear," said Fergie all at once, putting down her fork and taking up her teacup and holding it in both hands with the steam curling round, "you must remember just at fur-rst that yer Uncle Dur-rk and yer granny aren't used to children. I mean —" and Fergie put down the cup as if to think better how to say it — "they are kind, good people. Never mistake that! But yer uncle does have his moods, which you will just have to get used to and accept. And yer granny likes it quiet. That's why the phone's not listed —"

"I know," said Cory. "I tried to telephone —"

"— because Mrs. Van doesn't like just anybody calling," went on Fergie, "only her friends she's given the number to. And then she likes certain things to happen at certain times, and as for bur-rsting in on her — well, that ye wouldn't do, you understand, or tearing up and down stairs, or r-rampaging through the house like a young hurricane."

"Golly," said Peter, "I can rampage at home all I

want, or at least almost. But what'd I tell you, Cory? I *told* you I couldn't imagine anybody — well, I mean —" His voice trailed off.

"All the same," said Fergie, "ye seem like a quiet, well-behaved wee thing —"

"But I'll soon fix *that*," said Peter, grinning, with his green eyes full of mischief.

"Ye're a spalpeen, Peter, I'll wager — full of the Old Nick," accused Andrew, but his face lighted as if he liked that kind of boy better than any other.

"Now ye're just to leave the lassie alone, Peter!" exclaimed Fergie. "Right at fur-rst, anyway — about the r-rampaging. Her Uncle Dur-rk wouldn't mind so much, but it's —"

"Aye, it's the old lady," said Andrew darkly, as if he wasn't thinking what he was saying, but was speaking out of his heart.

At this Fergie blazed.

"Hush yer tongue, Andrew Ferguson! Ye'll frighten the child out of her wits —"

"*Me* frighten her!" cried Andrew, rearing up with his bronze eyes widening. "What about *you*? You started it all with yer, 'Och, yer Uncle Dur-rk this —' and 'Och, yer granny that —!' I don't know what ye're getting at *me* for —"

"Ah, well," said Fergie, subsiding and looking anxious and worried. "We'll just both hush, that's what we'll do. But after all, Cory dear, there's no use beating round the bush — ye'll just have to get used to them and they to you. That's the way of it. And now I'd better be seeing to yer room, and what ye should wear for the night. I think one of my nightgowns would do. And Peter, for the love of goodness — do get up her suitcase from the cave fur-rst thing in the morning —"

At that moment there came a knock at the door, and it was Peter's father, who was introduced to Cory and heard, in his turn, all about Peter's special, Explorer-type method of getting up to Tarnhelm. Then the two of them took themselves off into the windy, but no longer rainy, night, after Peter had gotten into the dry things his father had brought.

"See you tomorrow, Cory," he called out at the door. "Maybe I'll bring up *all* the Explorers — if I can round 'em up. Anyway, you'll get your suitcase!" And the door slammed.

After they had gone, it was quiet for a moment. Fergie was finishing her tea, Andrew had settled himself in one of the basket chairs near the stove, and Cory curled up in the other. She thought this one of the most satisfying rooms she'd ever been in, with its shining white tile around the sink and up behind the stove, the huge range with a place on the side where a wood fire was crackling, the table with its bright cloth, the blue and white braided rug underneath, and the large Welsh dresser nearby with its array of patterned plates. Though the kitchen was spacious, it was at the same time cozy and welcoming, and to Cory, after her long journey, it seemed the perfect place to be. She thought she could not possibly have been happier. She could hear the branches of oak and pine outside the windows swaying up and down in the wind, rubbing against one another; she could hear the rush of the wind and the muffled thunder of the sea, and thought all at once that she didn't care in the least if she never saw her grandmother and Uncle Dirk.

But what an awful thing to think! Immediately she took it back, especially about Uncle Dirk. Not to see either of them? They were her own family, and she had so little family.

"Well, there now," said Fergie, setting down her cup, "ye'd best be thinking of bed, Cory dear. It's after eight and ye've had a long, full day. Did ye know ye're to have Miss Stephanie's room? I must say I never thought to see a child in there — in fact, I never thought to see a child in this house. But it'll be good for it, and for everybody."

However, Cory had to tell them all about her flight on the jet, and so Fergie, with Cory's help, set about clearing the table and rinsing and stacking the dishes.

And then Andrew said he thought Cory should have a fire to go to sleep by.

"A *fire!* In my *room*, do you mean, Andrew?" she asked in blissful amazement. "You mean there's a *fireplace* in there?"

"Indeed, and why not?" demanded Andrew, filling up a box with paper and kindling and a small log or two from the big woodbin by the side of the stove. "Every one o' the bedrooms has a fireplace. There's central heating too, but yer granny and yer Uncle Dur-rk like their fires to go to bed by in the cold weather, and I don't blame them. Fergie and I have one in our sitting room — it's a delightful thing, a good blaze on a r-raw, blustery night to warm yer taes by." Cory knew he meant toes. She loved the way Fergie and Andrew talked.

Now off they went into the front realms of the house, along thick-carpeted hallways paneled smoothly in some light-toned wood on which paintings hung here and there, or dark carvings that seemed to be clusters of fruit and leaves, or masks whose features cast peaked shadows.

"As ye know, Cory, yer Uncle Dur-rk's an architect, but he's also been a woodcarver," said Fergie, "and a most gifted one, too. Have ye ever seen such beautiful masks?"

"I've never seen any at all," said Cory. "Not carved, I mean. Only Hallowe'en ones."

From the wide front hall, almost as large as a room, Cory caught a glimpse of the living room, where one or two lamps burned to welcome home the late-comers, and where rows of windows probably looked out over the winding road leading up to Tarnhelm and therefore over cliffs and sea to the west, and no doubt Peter's house too. How strange it will be to live here, thought Cory, after the apartment in New York. She and Stephanie (as she had told Peter) were to have had their own home, perhaps a little like this, but Stephanie had attempted too much. All the time Cory had spent in that house in Connecticut out in the hills during summer vacation, there had been nothing but tenseness, flare-ups at the workmen, fits of depression on Stephanie's part, interspersed with patches of complete happiness when the two of them went on picnics and rambles, and optimism that would flicker out again. They had lived like campers in an unfinished room while the rest of the house was being renovated, but had never moved out of it. Stephanie went on another tour to earn the money for bills that were mounting up, Cory went back to school, and the next thing she heard, Stephanie had sold the place.

Up on the second floor, she and Fergie and Andrew were going along a hall papered in rich blue, past one ivory door after another to a room with a large canopied four-poster bed where Cory was to sleep. She stared at it, and at the dresser with a long oval mirror in the center that took in the whole of you at one glance. There was a big desk where Cory promised herself she would write and write to her heart's content, and the fireplace with a deep-cushioned wing-back chair nearby. On each side of the fireplace were book shelves, and on the wall opposite as well, built up around the windows and with padded window seats underneath. When she saw the number of books there were, she could scarcely wait to find out what Stephanie had read "when she was my age," thought Cory. But there would be plenty of time for that.

"Did Grandmother and Uncle Dirk ever have any pets, Fergie?" she asked, as Fergie drew back the cream-colored bedspread, folded down the blankets and sheet into a neat V, and plumped the pillows.

"Aye, they did that," said Fergie. "Eight months ago, when Andrew and I fur-rst came, they had a pussy-cat named Biddy, a lovely, long-haired tabby she was, the sweetest-natured, most playful animal I have ever known in my life. Andrew and I loved that cat, and yer granny and Uncle Dur-rk too, and when

Biddy took some cat sickness and died, I thought yer granny would never get over it. She didn't speak for days."

"Did she cry, Fergie?"

"No, she did not," said Fergie briefly. "I have never known yer granny to cry."

"There ye are, lassie," said Andrew, stepping back from his handiwork. "How's that for a beauty?" Up leaped the flames, licking through the kindling and curling round the logs. "That'll last ye till long after ye're in dreamland."

"Imagine going to bed by firelight in a four-poster!" exclaimed Cory in delight. "Stephanie never told me about this bed — I don't know how she could have forgotten. I'll think about her being here, reading or getting ready for parties or writing letters, or sitting over there in the window seat looking down into the garden. I wonder if she had a cat — I must ask Grand-mother."

As Cory looked around the room, she noticed for the first time that a mask carved of some kind of honey-colored wood and hanging near the dressing table was of Stephanie. She went to it, put one hand up and with her finger traced the line of the brows, the perfectly straight, fine nose, the lips, the rounded chin. Though the face was not softened by Steph-anie's blond hair, and no eyes looked out, this *was*

Stephanie, even to that curious half-smile, a smile that often troubled Cory and made her uncertain. All at once she took down the mask and put it to her own face and looked through the eye-holes at her image in the mirror. She looked at her thin arms and legs, then took the mask away and studied her pale oval face and pointed chin, her dark eyes and black, thick, straight hair that hung to her shoulders and was cut in a bang across her forehead, an unruly bang which she kept pushing to the side.

"Is Grandmother beautiful, Fergie?"

"I should say she is a most handsome woman. I've never seen a handsomer."

"Does Stephanie look like her?"

"Yes — from that mask and from the pictures of Miss Stephanie I've seen, I should say they look very much alike."

"I wish I looked like Stephanie."

Fergie put her hand out to smooth Cory's hair.

"Why should ye want that, darling? I think ye're very fine as ye are, and I wouldn't want ye looking the least bit different."

"Well," said Cory, "I would really like to know if I look like my mother or my father. I've never seen a picture of either of them, not even a snapshot. And Stephanie won't talk about them because she says it makes her sad, so I don't ask. But I hope that maybe Grandmother'll have a picture and that she'll tell me about them. Shall I call her Grandmother, Fergie and Andrew, or would she prefer Granny, do you think, or maybe Grandma?"

"Oh, Gr-randmother, by all means!" exclaimed Andrew, drawing in his chin, with one eyebrow coming down and the other going right up. "I cannot imagine *anyone* calling Mrs. Van Heusen Granny."

"Well, we'll be off now — Andrew and I," said Fergie, "and ye'll away to yer bed, won't ye, Cory dear? Breakfast will be at eight-thirty if ye want to eat with yer family, or at seven if ye want to eat with us. I'll have yer clothes laid out all clean and ironed for you, so come down nice and neat, won't ye?"

Then, as if they had known her all their lives, or as if they were her grandmother and grandfather, they kissed her goodnight. "Sweet dreams!" Fergie wished her. "Aye, have a bonny sleep —" called out Andrew as they closed the door and went off down the hall. Cory stood for a moment in front of the fire, watching the flames, then quickly she went round all the book shelves. But what a disappointment! They were all old, dry, dull novels and histories and biographies of people she had never even heard of. It was as if there had been a great housecleaning and a whole load of books that had been overflowing the downstairs shelves had been put in here. At last, down under one of the window seats, Cory found all the Louisa May Alcott books and *The Five Little Peppers and How They Grew.*

"*The Five Little Peppers,*" she murmured. "It's been ages and ages —" She put it on the table beside the bed, turned out the lamp, then got into Fergie's nightgown and climbed in between the cold sheets that smelled faintly of lavender. She lay there watching the flames springing up and their flickering, dancing reflections on the wall and on the canopy above her head. Then she felt for her silver unicorn still hanging on its chain around her neck and held it in the palm of her left hand. If the unicorn were magical (and she believed it to be, though she had never said so to anyone), and she *were* bewitched or enchanted, because of being cawry-fisted, and if she wished on the unicorn, surely the combination of these two things should make any respectable wish come true.

"I wish," said Cory aloud, "I *wish* that Grandmother and Uncle Dirk will like me, and that they will want me to stay — at least for the rest of this term and summer vacation. And I wish that they will let me go to Peter's school and that the Explorers will take me in. But no matter what else happens, I wish that Grandmother and Uncle Dirk will like me."

Drowsily she thought that perhaps she might turn

on the lamp again and read in bed for ten or fifteen minutes. But before she could even reach up an arm, the unicorn had slipped from her fingers and she was asleep.

At some time during the night, Cory was half-awakened by a light shining in her face. A hand with a stone on one finger — a stone that flashed red, then peacock-colored fire—came out quickly to shade the light. She looked up in a daze and saw someone standing at her bedside, a tall woman with a straight, fine nose and dark eyes and white hair. There were little diamonds sparkling in her ears, Cory remembered afterwards, and there was a thick, silky-looking brown fur hanging in folds from her shoulders. She did not smile as she studied Cory but seemed thoughtful as she turned to someone standing at her side. Cory closed her eyes and had a feeling, after a little, that they had gone. But —

"— as I thought," she heard from far away, "a rather plain little thing —"

Then a man's voice:

"— get used to it, no doubt — won't last too long —"

Now the lamp was snapped off and Cory was dimly aware of their leaving the room and closing the door behind them.

Four

THE FIRST things she saw when she awoke were her suitcase and her train case standing there near the wing chair. Instantly she knew that the Explorers had already come and gone. What time was it? *Eight o'clock!* She threw back the blankets and ran to the window, pushed the casements open on a clean and shining morning, and stared anxiously into the garden for some sign of Peter and his friends. But there was only Andrew spading up the earth around the rose bushes and singing in a stirring baritone:

> *"Scots, wha hae wi' Wallace bled,*
> *Scots, wham Bruce has aften led,*
> *Welcome to yer gor-ry bed —"*

"Andrew! When did they come?"
By the desolation in her voice, Andrew did not

have to ask whom she meant. He leaned on his spade and squinted up at her.

"About six-thur-rty, I should say — only a minute or two after I was dressed and Fergie not even up yet."

"Did they say anything about coming back? Did Peter?"

"Not a wur-rd, lassie. They seemed in a great hurry. There's yer other suitcase on the porch, there. The Smallwoods came by with it just a wee bit ago."

She turned and ran into the hall and along beyond the staircase to a tall window at the end where she could get a full view of the water and the cliffs. Towering in the sky were dazzling clouds full of blue-shadowed entrance-ways and vast snowy terraces, and the sun shone on such an ocean as you think of when you say, "Calm seas and happy voyage —" with white rollers creaming on the sand and gulls bobbing on the waves.

But as for human beings, there were none. Not a soul. Cory studied the group of oaks at the distant end of the lawn where, just beyond, the ravine began. But no children played there, either in the deep shade or along the branches, half-hidden by leaves. They must be far away by now, engaged in their own private and fascinating business, with the whole perfect day ahead of them. By the heaviness of her dis-

appointment, Cory knew she had been planning on getting up early enough to welcome them and perhaps even inveigling Fergie into letting them stay for breakfast. Thus they could all have gotten acquainted, she and Fergie and Andrew with the Explorers, and that would have been the opening wedge.

Well, she would just have to think up something else.

On the dot of eight-thirty she came into the breakfast room, which she had passed the night before. She stood at the doorway for a moment, looking first at

Uncle Dirk and then at her grandmother. But these were not the Wicked Queen and the Black Prince! They looked up smiling, one at each end of the table with the bright, sun-speckled windows between them, opposite Cory. She knew from Stephanie that Uncle Dirk was only twenty-nine, but he looked older, she thought, with deep-set eyes even darker than her own, heavy eyebrows, the rather prominent Van Heusen nose, and a sprinkling of gray already beginning to show in his black hair.

"*Hel*-lo, Cory," he said, just exactly as she knew he would. "I see you got your beauty sleep."

For some reason she could not find a word to say in answer.

Grandmother Van Heusen, erect, dignified, and indeed, as Fergie had said, handsome, with shining white hair and dark eyes like her son's, was holding out her arm.

"Good morning, Cory dear. Welcome to Tarnhelm. Did you have a good night's rest after your strange day yesterday? I'm so sorry everything got mixed up — otherwise you know we'd have been there to meet you."

Cory went to her and slipped a quick, shy kiss onto the leaf-smooth cheek, thinking, as she pressed close, how fresh and fragrant her grandmother smelled. Then she went round and got the hug and kiss from Uncle Dirk she had thought about on the plane and also when she had stood waiting for him to come — not just the hug and kiss, but the whole moment of welcome. Yet how different from what she had imagined. He's shy too — like me, thought Cory, but his eyes rested warmly on her as she sat down between them, facing the windows where pine branches moved in the wind, and he seemed amused at something.

"So you've been rescued by a knight-errant already," he said, "and you've only just arrived. That's a good beginning —"

"Do you mean Peter, Uncle Dirk?" began Cory,

when Fergie whisked in, set down a platter of scrambled eggs and bacon and seemed to have to move a lot of dishes and clink silver around.

"The walk through the rain he means, darling," she said quickly. "Those Smallwoods running out of gas, again — would ye believe it! — and at such an unfortunate time, too. However, it was very kind of them to bring her, and Andrew thanked them when they came by with her other case." She pressed Cory's shoulder, gave her a bright look and went out, leaving, Cory noticed, the kitchen door just slightly ajar.

"But I don't understand why Peter didn't take you directly to his own house, Cory," said Mrs. Van Heusen. "It would have been only a few minutes away from the main road and you wouldn't have been caught in the storm and gotten your shoes ruined. I think I must speak to him — I wouldn't want him thinking —"

"Oh, Grandmother, *please!* You see, maybe sometime I could join the Explorers. I've never been in a club, and they've all done something difficult and courageous, and they'd *never* take me in if you got after Peter about bringing me here in the storm."

Mrs. Van Heusen was quiet for a moment.

"Well, of course, I must do as I think best, Cory."

"Yes, I know. I *know* you must. But I have got to learn to hike and climb and swim as quick as I can, because I'll never get in without that, and maybe Peter'll teach me but he wouldn't if he thought I was — I mean, if he thought you —"

Mrs. Van Heusen buttered a piece of toast and spread on a trace of jam. Her pink enameled nails shone like speckless shells and the stone on her finger burned a deep fiery red, then green — or was it blue? "Cory, I think that for your own sake we must get something straight at once. You're to be here only a short time — not indefinitely, I mean — and we can't have you doing difficult and courageous things. Foolhardy, dangerous things, they could be. We can't send you back to Stephanie in pieces, and we can't — Fergie and I — be put to the worry of constantly wondering what you're up to. Surely you understand?"

Cory took this in.

"You mean I'm not to do *anything*, Grandmother? Not go *anywhere* with the Explorers — or by myself?"

"I feel you should be sensible, Cory. That's all I ask."

There was a flat silence, then all at once Uncle Dirk leaned over and put his hand on her arm.

"I tell you what. I'll teach you to swim — how's that? And we'll make Peter's eyes pop if you learn fast enough. You'll have to, in any case. Learn fast, I mean."

66

She gazed at him in relieved astonishment.

"Oh, Uncle Dirk — would you?" But then —

"Dirk, what are you getting the child into? You'll only make it more difficult for her." Mrs. Van Heusen looked straight at him, but he only grinned at her. And Cory, overjoyed, spread so much butter and jam on her toast that she saw Mrs. Van Heusen wince. "Did you mind leaving Stephanie?" her grandmother asked, as if to change the subject for now, but intending to speak to Uncle Dirk later. "I should think she misses you when she goes away, Cory."

"But how could she when she's so busy? She's away a lot of the time on tour, but that's all right," Cory said lightly, imagining this to be true because the present seemed so full of promise. "It's not as if I don't understand how things are between Stephanie and me. She's a professional, and so she's different from most people and I can't expect it to be any other way. In fact, at the airport we had a talk about it. She said she had something she's been meaning to tell me for ages, and she started in about —"

"Good!" said Mrs. Van Heusen. She put down her coffee cup and rested her elbows on the table with her two hands clasped together and a look on her face as if she were going to say the truth. "Now I'm thankful Stephanie has finally decided to get on with the adoption. I've never understood why she didn't do it long ago, but Stephanie has always hated legal details — having to take time out from her work. I've never known anyone so consumed —"

Cory knew Fergie was standing right behind her. But everything else slid right away in the midst of a queer silence. She felt hollow in her middle, and cold and yet burning hot all at the same time. She stared down at something that dazzled — then up, first at her grandmother coming slowly into focus, then at Uncle Dirk.

"I didn't know. Stephanie didn't tell me. That's what I was going to say — that she started in about something, but then the plane came. I thought I *was* adopted — I thought I've *always* been. You mean I'm not?"

Now Fergie went around the table to the other side and grasped the coffee pot, her blue gaze fixed upon Cory. Uncle Dirk sat there and studied his mother with his jaw set and his face unreadable, and he didn't say anything at all. As for Mrs. Van Heusen, she sat stiffly, her nose pinched as a bone, as if someone had slapped her or as if she were mortally offended.

"This is unforgivable," she said, and put one hand across her eyes. "I can't believe it! Why, Stephanie *told* me in her last letter —" Then she looked at Cory. "Don't cry, child. It doesn't make any difference, really."

68

"I'm not going to cry. But it *does* make a differ-ence, Grandmother. It *does*. If I'm — if I'm not adopted, then I don't belong. I don't belong any-where —"

"Nonsense!" said Uncle Dirk. "You belong right here."

"I mean I don't have any family."

"We're your family," he said.

"But not really — not *really*. If Stephanie adopted me, *then* you'd be. But she didn't — *why* didn't she? *Why-y-y-?*" and Cory's voice, out of control all at once without warning, went up and up and her throat burned with a paining fierceness. She felt Fergie's hands on her shoulders and presently she got out in a queer, shaking voice she hated, "I wish you'd tell me about my parents. If you know anything about them, I wish you'd tell me. Stephanie never will — and I've asked her."

There was another silence, and now Fergie's hands slid away and the kitchen door closed behind her.

"We're in the soup anyway," said Uncle Dirk after a bit. "Besides, why shouldn't she know about her own parents? Though there's very little to tell, Cory. I don't know why Stephanie wouldn't."

"Please tell me the very little."

"Yes, Dirk," said Mrs. Van Heusen with sudden firmness. "Tell the child. And we shall just face

Stephanie. This whole thing has been horribly un-
fair —"

"Well, Cory," began Uncle Dirk, and she turned
to him, leaning forward, her shoulders sloping and her
hands clasped in her lap, her eyes fixed on his face,
her whole being focused, "your parents, as Stephanie
may at least have told you, were her very dear friends
Lawrence and Coralie Winterslow. They'd been
friends of hers long before they were married, even,
and they'd go skiing together whenever Stephanie was
home and it was the season, and they came and
stayed with her in New York after they were married.
Then they moved to England —"

"To *England?*" repeated Cory.

"Oh, yes," said Uncle Dirk, "to London, in fact.
And while they were living there, they had a baby —"

"Me," said Cory.

"Yes, you. And I remember the address because
Stephanie wrote us once or twice from their house,
and I always liked the sound of it: Number 7, Swans
Lake Walk, Crescent Gardens, London, W.C.2."

"Number 7, Swans Lake Walk, Crescent Gardens,
London, W.C.2." said Cory to herself. She saw it, a
small, dignified house surrounded by trees, and there
were two figures at the gate in front it, a man and a
woman, and beside them a nurse in a white starched

70

cap and apron, and there was a baby in the nurse's arms.

"When you were about three," went on Uncle Dirk, "your parents all at once decided they wanted to go to Switzerland and go skiing and climbing again. Stephanie was there, and they hadn't been over since before you were born, though they'd climbed in the Scottish mountains — the Grampians. I don't know exactly what happened, Cory, but a few days after they arrived at the hotel, your parents and Stephanie went out with the guide for a climb, and I believe your mother and father were knocked into a crevasse by a snow slide. They couldn't get to your father, but they brought your mother down to the hotel and she asked Stephanie to take you, because your father's parents were dead and there was no one in her own family she wanted to leave you with. That's all we know — that's absolutely all."

Cory sat without moving, taking in all of Uncle Dirk's words, seeing the enormous white peaks, the little figures struggling upward, and then the snow coming down.

"Thank you, Uncle Dirk, for telling me. Do you have any pictures of them? Did Stephanie ever send any?"

"No, dear," said Mrs. Van Heusen. "No, I'm sorry, she never did."

Shortly after this, Cory went upstairs. She went into her room and stood staring at the mask of Stephanie, whose little half-smile seemed now more enigmatic than ever. She had thought she would come up here and cry in peace with nobody watching, but found that she had no desire to. Stephanie could, whenever she pleased, so that it sent you all to pieces, and the whole time she was only acting. Yet there were the real tears running down her face and that look in her eyes and her chest going up and down, and then she'd smile at you right in the midst of them and you knew she'd been fooling. But you never could tell ahead of time.

Cory went over and got up on the bed and pulled the curtains to, all the way around. Then she lay face down trying to think everything out and what she must do. She had no idea how long she lay there, but presently someone knocked at the bedroom door, then came in. It was Fergie, and she sat down on the bed and laid a cool hand against Cory's cheek.

"Did you know, Fergie?"

"Yes, my lamb, if you mean did I know you hadn't been adopted yet. But of course, from what yer granny said about Miss Stephanie's last letter, I thought it had all been gone through before ye came out here. It never occurred to me it hadn't."

"Fergie, what am I to do? I've got to do something.

I've *got* to know why Stephanie won't adopt me. Maybe there's a reason. Do you suppose she promised my mother she would?"

There was a short silence, and then Fergie said:

"Ye must write her. Ye must sit down now and write her the whole truth, and ask her what ye have to know. It's the only way to put yourself at rest."

"Do you think Grandmother and Uncle Dirk would mind? Uncle Dirk said they'd be in the soup for telling —"

"Well, I shall ask them, and if I don't come up again, ye'll know it's all right."

After Fergie had gone, Cory got some paper from her suitcase and a pen from her purse and sat down at Stephanie's desk.

Dear Stephanie:

Here I am at Tarnhelm in your room with the four-poster bed with the top on it, and the curtains you can pull around, and I do like the fireplace and the bookshelves and everything. But now I know that you still haven't adopted me and I wonder why. Because of what you wrote Grandmother she thought for sure you'd finally told me and so she went ahead and talked about it. I guess that was what you were going to tell me before I got on the plane — I have a feeling it was because you acted so funny then releeved when the plane came. Please, Stephanie, write right away and tell me why you haven't. How can I belong? I felt so awful, that Uncle Dirk told me about my parents and about number 7 Swans Lake Walk and about how they went to Switzerland to meet you and how they were climbing and what happened and now I know why you always said it made you sad and I'm sorry but I feel better knowing. If you have a picture of them would you send it to me and a picture of number 7? I can see it in my mind but probly its very different. And tell me why you haven't adopted me because its *awfully important!!* Please write me as soon as you possibly can because I have got to know.

Love from Cory

P.S. I hope you are having a success.

Now she had only to find Stephanie's forwarding address in London, which she had somewhere in her purse. But no sooner had she got it and addressed an envelope she found in the desk drawer than there came a rap at the door.

"I have a little time, Cory," said Uncle Dirk, "and I thought you might like to go down to the beach for a swimming lesson."

Cory sat there with the letter in her hand, trying to decide what to say. Uncle Dirk was wanting to be kind; he wanted to make up to her for what had happened. Yet, now, learning to swim, that had seemed

so important when she was happy, made no difference at all.

"You mean right this minute, Uncle Dirk?"

"As soon as you get into your suit. You brought
one, I suppose."

"Yes —"

"Well, it's all right if you don't want to —"

"But I do — I'll get ready. I'll be ready in two
shakes. Thanks for asking me."

In the car, Uncle Dirk put her letter into the glove
compartment and said that he would go right to the
post office and mail it the minute he got into town.

"We won't have very long on the beach because
I have friends coming, but we'll have long enough.
And it's better for you to be outside doing something."

She looked up at him, watching his face and wondering what was going through his head, for now he
seemed lost in thought as they wound down curve
after curve from the heights of Tarnhelm toward the
entrance with its carved sign. He seemed closed away.
"I saw the sign you made, Uncle Dirk, and the unicorn. And when I saw that I knew Peter must be
wrong."

But what was she saying! Her face went scarlet
with embarrassment because now she would have to
explain why she'd known Peter was wrong and what

had led up to it. However, Uncle Dirk seemed not to have heard, for he made no reply; but after what seemed a long time, he lifted his head.

"You knew Peter must be wrong about what, Cory? In what way? What difference did the unicorn make?"

"Unicorns are magic," she said in a muffled voice. "And I thought that if you liked unicorns enough to carve one at the entrance to Tarnhelm, then I was sure Peter must be mistaken about you —"

"How mistaken?"

"Well — he said you saw him on the cliffs and that you shouted at him to get off your property. He said you seemed angry when really he wasn't doing anything —"

"And he told you when he brought you here that he was glad he wasn't coming to stay — was that it?" Uncle Dirk gave a chuckle. "Well, I was probably thinking that Peter would fall into the sea and that I'd have to go and fish him out, and I hadn't time to get boys out of the sea just then."

Cory knew that he hadn't resented her confession.

"Maybe," she said, "on that day you were the Black Prince."

"And other days?"

"Other days you're Uncle Dirk, the one who wrote to me."

Five

HE PARKED his car not far from Peter's house
(Cory was certain it must be Peter's — a vine-covered
shingled house near the cliffs with a terrace on the
seaward side protected by a low stone wall). Then he
led the way through the trees to a flight of steep
wooden steps leading down to the beach Peter had
told her about. For the first time since breakfast, on
seeing the long, white, curving beach with its upthrust
of dark rocks at one end, Cory felt her heart lighten.
She felt it quicken with excitement at sight of the gulls
wheeling high up, being blown in the wind and then
planing down on still wings, and the green waves beneath them hurtling in and curving over. She had not
often been to any beach, for Maureen McQueeny
had been with them only during the winter and no
other lady-help they had ever had was the least interested in eating picnics on the sand ("dirty, gritty busi-

77

ness") or going near the sea, least of all at Coney Island. Now the fresh, stinging, salt-smelling wind blew against her. She snuffed it, her nose wrinkled and her eyes squinted against the brilliance of sea and sky with the sunlight dancing along the crests of the waves as though gold foil had been cut out in zigzags.

The beach was deserted, which seemed to please Uncle Dirk, and at the bottom of the steps he took her hand and made her run almost faster than she could manage across the sand. He threw off his robe near the wave-line, and when Cory tossed down hers and stood there in her brand new coral bathing suit, he put out his hand and lifted up the little silver unicorn hanging on its chain. He held it, turned it over, then looked at her.

"Did you have this on at breakfast?" He seemed surprised he hadn't noticed it.

"Oh, yes — I always do. It was prob'ly down inside my collar. I've had it ever since I can remember. Stephanie told me it was my mother's." Still he stood there, seeming to be thinking, smoothing it with his thumb. "That's why I was happy when I saw yours on the sign. Do unicorns mean something special to you too, Uncle Dirk?"

"Yes," he said. "Ever since I was a boy they have. I loved British history, and all the kings and pomp and ceremonies, and when I came to heraldry I couldn't

78

have enough of it. I thought 'blazoned' the most splendid word in the world and I was fascinated by crescents and chiefs and fesses and bends and foils and fleur-des-lys —"

"And lions and unicorns fighting for the crown," put in Cory, "and the lion beat the unicorn all around the town —"

"Yes, and I pestered my friends for details about their families so that I could make crests for them whether they wanted me to or not —"

"And you made one for the Van Heusens?"

"Oh, they already had theirs, and Mother's family too, of course — the Stewarts. But I worked out a joint coat-of-arms that was really pretty handsome as I remember it. Anyway, what I meant to tell you: when I was back east one spring and went up to see Stephanie, I met your mother and father in her apartment — that was just before they went to England — and I noticed particularly that your father had on a silver unicorn tie pin and your mother this little unicorn on a chain around her neck. I'm glad you have it."

"But the other one, Uncle Dirk? The other unicorn on the tie pin? Where do you suppose it is? I've never seen it."

"Given away and probably lost long ago," he said shortly, and turned and went down the beach into

the sea, and all the gulls flapped up, creeing and crying in a cloud. He plunged into the surf and dived
without stopping under an incoming wave that swallowed him in its cavernous green mouth, and he came
out on the far side as sleek and lively as a fish.

Oh, thought Cory with half her mind, I wish I
could do that! But with the other half she wondered
why Stephanie hadn't given her her father's tie pin as
well and told herself to be sure and ask.

She went carefully into the surf, but the instant it
frothed around her feet, she shuddered. It was so
bitingly cold that she ran out, shocked, and then, seeing Uncle Dirk waving to her to try again, went hesi-
tantly back.

"All at once!" he shouted to her. "You've got to
get in all at —" and the rest was lost.

All at once? But I can't — I can't! She crouched
down, waiting for the water to surge around her, and
the instant it rose against her legs, her teeth clenched
and every muscle in her stomach contracted into a
knot. Now Uncle Dirk was swimming strongly, far
out, and while he was gone she tried again and again
to get in at least as far as her knees.

And finally, though the cold was painful as fire, she
managed, when a somewhat smaller wave came surg-
ing in, to let it sweep around her. But down she went
in the swift backwash. Over and over it tumbled her

on the scouring, sandy bottom as if she had been a stone. Now the next wave smothered her and every time she managed barely to catch her breath she was smacked flat until she no longer knew what was happening to her. She caught a flash of blue sky and horizon of cliffs all crazily tilted with bits of white sweeping across the blinding sun, and once, even, a blurred glimpse of Peter's house and thought vaguely what a shame it was that she would never have a chance to go there nor ever to see him again or get to know the Explorers. A new wave reared up — she saw its jade-green dome from the inside with yellow light piercing the crest as if she were under a luminous bowl. It descended on her head, she went down into blinding blackness until — all at once — an arm came round her, she was hauled onto the beach, and there was Uncle Dirk laughing in her face.

"You were supposed to wait! I only wanted you to get wet —"

She could not breathe. She could only stare at him like a pale, blubbering, gaping fish, and she was shaking so hard she couldn't even answer him — not only shaking with cold but with the most shaming fear she had ever known. She could not go in again. She *could not.* And she would never, never learn to swim and Peter and Uncle Dirk would be absolutely disgusted with her.

But he did not seem to be in the least disgusted. He got the big, thick towel he had brought and rubbed her so hard she thought her skin was coming off, and when a warm glow began to flow through her, she started laughing.

"I meant to wait," she said.

"You forgot to put one hand around your unicorn."

"But if I hadn't had it," said Cory, "you'd never have found me."

"Nonsense — do you think I didn't have an eye on you?" He rubbed himself dry, and when she put her robe on they sat down and watched the birds and the sea. But it seemed he could not sit still for long.

"I have to be going, Cory, but you stay for a while if you like and wander around and explore until lunchtime."

"Could I go back along Peter's trail where you saw him, or would I have to go back all that long way up the road?"

"The kids have been taking that trail ever since I was a boy," said Uncle Dirk. "I've been along it hundreds of times — just be careful and watch where you're going." He unfolded himself and looked down at her. "We have to trust you, Cory. You've got to learn to be careful and use your common sense, because Fergie and Andrew can't be watching out for you the whole time, *nor* Peter. And certainly not your grandmother and I." He reached out and roughed up her hair. "Get back at lunchtime — Fergie'll be expecting you."

He started off across the sand, and in a moment Cory was tearing after him.

"Uncle Dirk, you'll send my letter to Stephanie airmail special delivery —"

"I will. I promise you faithfully I will."

After he had gone, Cory explored the whole beach, keeping a watch on Peter's house to see if she might catch sight of him, but he did not appear. Gradually, she began humming to herself as she searched for treasures. She found a small bleached bird's skull, ivory-colored and perfect and not in the least fragile. She found a curiously shaped piece of driftwood with peaked shells clinging to it, and another shell among a pile of seaweed. It was oval, like a little saucer, a rough, dull greeny-yellow, the precise color of the seaweed to which it was stuck. But when she finally managed to pry it off and turned it over, she discovered that on the inside it was glistening smooth as glass, pearly around the outside and with a pool of rich color in the center like frozen sea water. She put her treasures in a safe place, then went down near the surf in among the tall black rocks and made up a play of danger and suspense and courage with herself as the heroine. And she was so lost in it, hidden among the rocks where nobody could see her talking to herself and making faces and taking dramatic poses, that she was astonished when she came out and found the entire beach changed.

The sea was hung with a golden mist and now everything was quiet, as though the beach were asleep and did not want to be disturbed — or as if Something slept, and the waves, smaller than they had been, lapped in without a sound and fell — hush-sh-sh-sh — all up and down the shore. Gulls wheeled with never a cry, lighting with a final lifting of the wings, then folded them in neatly and stood gazing seaward at that strange vision of an enormous shape in an enormous boat rowing and rowing in and never arriving. Of course it was only a pelican on a log, and it was the mist did it — turned even that figure up on the cliff above her into a towering giant.

Cory leaned over a washed-in plank with a nail sticking up to reach for a colored pebble in the sand. And as she drew back, the unicorn chain caught on the nail and snapped, and the chain flew off — where she did not see. Horror-stricken, she searched desperately. But the chain was so fine, and the unicorn so small, that if it had fallen into a hollow of sand and she had stepped near in her search, it could easily have been buried forever.

"Where can it be — where can it be?" she cried softly to herself.

"Where can what be?" asked a voice.

Cory looked up and there stood a young woman in shorts and a gray-blue pull-over sweater, with her brown hair falling around her shoulders. She knelt down beside Cory and repeated her question. "Where can what be? What is it you've lost?"

"My unicorn! I've *got* to find it. I've had it all my life —"

"Can this be it?" And the young woman reached over, not a foot from Cory's hand, and drew from the sand the little unicorn on its chain. But when she saw it, she held it with her fingers curved round as it lay in her palm, looking at it for a moment while Cory watched her, overcome with relief.

"Where did you get it?"

"It was my mother's, and Stephanie, the person I live with, gave it to me."

"Oh. Well, now, you must get someone to take a pair of pliers and press that little link there, near the clasp, together again so that you'll be sure not to lose it. But let me see, what will you do with it meanwhile?

Here —" and the young woman forced the two ends of the link together again with her teeth and then put the chain around Cory's neck.

"Thank you ever so much! My name's Cory Winterslow. What's yours?"

"Laurel," said the young woman. "Laurel Woodford."

"Laurel Woodford! Why, that name just suits you, because do you know why? You look like a dryad, and a laurel is a kind of tree, isn't it? And then Woodford — it all fits together. And do you know something else about names? When Andrew and Fergie saw that I was left-handed last night, they said my name was just right for me, because cawry-fisted means left-handed in Scotland. And they said because of that I'm either bewitched or enchanted or both, whichever's best. Do you know the difference?"

"If you're bewitched, you've had a spell put on you," said Laurel, "and I think being enchanted is the same. Who are Fergie and Andrew?"

Cory told her about them, and why she loved them, and then about coming to stay with her uncle and grandmother while Stephanie was away on tour.

"Of course, Uncle Dirk's liable to have moods, Fergie said, and Grandmother's not used to having children around. But I think it'll be all right. Except there's been kind of a difficulty about Stephanie. So I've written her a letter to find out about it." Cory looked down and drew a line in the sand and then put circles around it. "We sent the letter air-mail special delivery." She looked up and there was Laurel studying her.

"I hope it turns out all right for you, Cory," she said. "Somehow or other."

"Perhaps I'll see you again and so then I can tell you. Do you come here often?"

"Not now. I used to, when I was a child and growing up, but hardly at all any more."

Cory got the bird skull and the piece of driftwood and the shell. "I'm going to keep them because I found them on my first morning on the beach."

Laurel pointed to them one by one.

"The little shells on the driftwood are called owl limpets, and the large shell is a pearly monia. I found one of those on a specially happy morning on this very beach. The skull is a turnstone's, I think, or a sandpiper's. Isn't it wonderfully put together?" She smiled at Cory.

> *"Nothing of him that doth fade*
> *But doth suffer a sea-change*
> *Into something rich and strange.*

Sea-nymphs hourly ring his knell:
Hark! Now I hear them — Ding, dong, bell."

"Did you make that up?" Cory asked.

"No, Shakespeare did, for *The Tempest*. There, that's my friend calling me. Cooo-eee!" called up Laurel toward the bluffs behind them. "I'm coming —! I must go now, Cory, but I hope we'll see each other again. Shall we drive you home?"

"Oh, it's not far off if I go along the path Peter showed me. And I want to stop by his house."

"Good luck, then. Goodbye — I'll be thinking about you."

But when she was gone and Cory went through the mist up to Peter's house, she was almost too shy to knock at the door. When she finally gathered courage and it opened, a woman stood there — Mrs. Hawthorne, this must be, thought Cory.

No, Peter wasn't at home, Mrs. Hawthorne said. He'd gone off with his friends. They had a club called the Explorers.

"Oh, I *know*. Would you tell him when he comes back that Cory Winterslow was here? I wanted to thank him for bringing my suitcase up, and the train case."

"I'll tell him, dear. He and the rest of them were

88

having a meeting when you got knocked down by the wave."

For the second time that day, Cory blushed scarlet. They had been watching her — the whole Explorers Club!

"Oh, don't feel badly," laughed Mrs. Hawthorne. "Do you imagine you're the only one who's ever been knocked down by a wave? I should say not. Would you like to come in? Though I'm afraid the Explorers have gone off for the rest of the afternoon — they took their lunches with them."

"I think," said Cory, "I'd better be getting home if it's afternoon. Fergie will be looking for me."

"Watch going through the fog, then, dear," said Mrs. Hawthorne, and the door closed as Cory turned and went back across the terrace.

What fun it would have been to have "gone off for the rest of the afternoon." And with their lunches! Would she ever go with them? What did they do, do you suppose? Where did they go? What did they talk about? Cory sighed, tightened the belt of her robe, made certain she had all her treasures, and followed on down the path that snaked through the bushes toward the trail along the cliffs.

It was not until she came to the cave and leaned over to look inside in case there should be someone or something hiding in there that she noticed that her head hurt. And when she straightened up again she felt so dizzy that she thought it would be better to sit down for a moment. When she finally got up and went on, inside a little gray room that moved along with her as she moved, she felt hot, which was odd on such a cool day. For now the sun was hidden entirely and the mist was no longer golden but thick and damp and clinging. She ached as she climbed up the steep bank toward the wall at the foot of the lawn she and Peter had run across only last night in the pouring rain.

"Cory!" called Fergie from the porch. "Where on ear-rth have ye been, lassie? I was expecting ye long before now."

Cory did not run across the grass this time, because when she bobbed up and down her head hurt worse than ever. But she did not say anything to Fergie in case she might feel better later on, and if Peter came she wanted to be able to eat dinner, if he were asked to stay, without anybody asking questions or fussing about her.

"Am I late, Fergie?"

"Oh, no, not really. It's only a quarter of one — I was just wondering. My, what red cheeks! Did ye have fun?"

She tried to tell Fergie and Andrew at lunch all that had happened during the morning, and she wanted specially to tell them about Laurel Woodford and about the peculiar feeling of the beach when it became so still, and how Laurel found her unicorn as if by magic. But she found that she could not eat, nor get up any energy to talk, and presently she said:

"Fergie, I think I'd better go upstairs."

Fergie gave her one quick, keen, piercing look, pressed her palm to Cory's forehead, and got up.

"Come along, then, darling," she said, and Cory saw her glance at Andrew and draw in her chin.

Six

CORY knew that she slept off and on for the rest of the afternoon and was dimly aware that people came and went, came again, and stood by the bed looking down at her. Someone took her temperature. No, twice someone took it — first she thought it was Fergie, and then a man she didn't know, who had a low voice and gentle hands, and he gave her a chocolatey medicine, the taste of which stayed in her mouth unpleasantly for a long time afterwards. She knew that Uncle Dirk and Mrs. Van Heusen came in, but that was much later, when it was getting dark. Then the lamp on the night stand was turned on and something put over it so that it shone softly, and after that she thought that nobody but Fergie came and she was sure it was night — very late, but her lamp was still on.

The next thing, it seemed to her that its subdued light had changed to the luminous fog on the beach, with the sun a veiled globe trying to shine through. Of course she was dreaming, but it was all very real. She was talking to Laurel Woodford again, telling her that she had left something of the greatest importance out of her letter — no, two things. But what were they? She should have written them on the back of the envelope, though they were private and Stephanie wouldn't have wanted them written where everybody could see. There was something Uncle Dirk had told her —

"And who is Uncle Dirk?" asked Laurel.

"Dirk Van Heusen — he lives right up there," and Cory turned to point through the fog to where Tarnhelm stood on the headland above the sea, but it wasn't there. No houses at all were there, not Peter's nor anyone's. And when Cory turned back to tell Laurel that it must be the fog working some trick, she too had vanished, and she knew it was Stephanie there instead, though she was invisible through the thick mist. Then Stephanie laughed, that little amused laugh of hers.

"Cory, you know perfectly well you haven't fulfilled the requirements."

For her to adopt me, Cory thought.

"But what requirements, Stephanie? What must I do?"

"You can't hike any distance at all, or climb or

swim, even — and you know you'll never be able to swim now —"

There was nothing to be heard but the sea — or was that the sea? It was making a strange sort of music, like drops of water falling in grave, slow measures, now faint and faraway, then stronger again. She felt sick and confused and not at all herself. Could she still be dreaming? She wasn't sure; she knew only that her head hurt like fury and that she was desperately thirsty. There was a light — was it the moon? — that seemed a pinpoint, then it drew near until it became frighteningly huge, then receded again. Nothing was itself. She wanted a drink, but she wanted above all to find where the music was coming from. There was something about it, something haunting and sad that made her long to hear it more clearly. She was sure that when she found it, there she would find Laurel — or was it Stephanie she was searching for? In her troubled confusion she couldn't be certain.

She went along a dark hallway where the music sounded more loudly until she came to a half-open door. Here she went in and pushed out the casement and listened, but no — now the music was fainter than before. Not far off on her right was another door, and when she opened it and went along a short hall, she found that a flight of steps led downward.

At the bottom she found herself in a great, high-ceilinged room furnished in the queerest way with clumps of furniture in some places and then vast stretches with no furniture at all. Brilliant shafts of moonlight fell through a series of windows, and under some of these were cabinets. But it was too dark for Cory to see what was in them, and she did not want to lean over in case it made her so dizzy that she would not be able to find her way out of the big room again. She went toward one of the windows where the moonlight was pouring in and opened it and listened.

As she reached up to pull back the casement, she noticed that on the cabinet underneath there stood a chess set partly arranged on its board. The rest of the pieces were in a carved box, and as she lifted them out, one by one, she saw by the moonlight that some of them had faces. So finely and precisely were they carved that when Cory ran her fingers over the faces of the bishops and kings and queens, the light and the dark, she could feel their little noses and lips and chins and the hollows of their eyes. They had tiny hands upheld. They seemed to be dressed in a medieval way, and the folds of their garments were smooth as if each piece had been rubbed to a gloss. The kings and queens had crowns on their heads, each one different, and the bishops had miters. The castles were real castle towers with long, narrow windows and crenellated tops. But most surprising of all were the four knights.

Instead of horses' heads (which she knew these pieces usually are), they were unicorns, rearing up on their hind legs with their forefeet pawing the air, their necks curved, their little ears forward, and a single, straight horn spiraling from the center of each forehead. What especially delighted Cory was the feeling

of verve and spirit in them, each in a different position. They seemed truly magical to her, as if they might move in her hand at any moment, their heads toss back and their hoofs start dancing. She told herself that if she were ever to play with such a set, she would hardly be able to keep her mind on the game for making up stories for the kings and queens and knights and bishops and pawns to act out.

She hated to put them back, yet felt more sick and feverish than ever and knew that she must go. Then she decided not to put them in the box again, but to leave them standing on the board so that they could continue, the moment she left, with whatever adventure they might have been in the midst of.

She wanted to take them with her, but dared not for some reason, and so turned and made her way back to the stairs and climbed up. After this she became lost and wandered about miserably in the dark for a long time trying to find where she had first heard the music — the grave, slow, sad music whose notes had fallen clearly like drops of water.

The next thing she knew, there was Fergie leaning over her, laying a hand against her cheek and then on her forehead.

"Ye wee spalpeen! Do ye know what time it is?"

Cory had no idea.

"It's two in the afternoon!"

This was enormously puzzling, and she frowned and shut her eyes.

"But I thought we'd just had dinner — I mean — you were eating, or was that lunch? And I had to come upstairs because I felt so sick —"

Now another long stretch of time twisted away, during which Fergie would come in and give her something cool to drink and take her temperature and go out again, and Cory tossed and flopped and got the bed all rumpled because first she shivered and then had to throw the blankets off.

At last, out of a deep sleep, she opened her eyes and there were Uncle Dirk and Mrs. Van Heusen standing at the foot of the bed.

"But I thought you weren't home yet," said Cory.

"Listen to her!" cried Fergie, coming over from the door. "That was the night before last, darling. Ye've been sleeping all night and all day, and all night and all day, right round the clock until now. Ye chattered and had a fever of a hundred and three, then ye calmed down about ten this morning and ye've been peaceful as a lamb ever since. I think ye're going to be just fine."

"A bit pale and thin," said Uncle Dirk consideringly, "but much better." He looked extremely relieved.

Mrs. Van Heusen came and laid her hand lightly on Cory's forehead just as Fergie had done. "You had us *quite* worried, Cory dear." She drew up a chair and sat there leaning forward. "How do you feel?"

"All right." How comforting it was to have everybody gathered around and asking about her. But there was something she wanted to ask Uncle Dirk, something bothering and unhappy. "Uncle Dirk, I dreamed about my letter and I could have asked Stephanie to tell me about the other unicorn — the one on the tie pin — on the outside of the envelope. Did you mail it?"

"Just as I promised. Air-mail special delivery."

"And I forgot the most important thing of all. I didn't ask Stephanie if she hasn't adopted me because she doesn't really *want* to. Do you suppose that could be it?"

Mrs. Van Heusen shook her head.

"No, Cory, I do not. She probably has some reason we have no inkling of, but I'm absolutely certain that is not it."

Cory thought this over, then frowned, because there was one more thing she wanted to get straight.

"Uncle Dirk, what did you mean when you and Grandmother came in after I was asleep the first night I was here? I thought you said you'd get used to having me here — no doubt — as if you didn't really think you would, but that my visit wouldn't last too long."

Uncle Dirk stared at her, then he laughed.

"What a lot of thinking you've been doing while you were sick. But I didn't say that at all — at least I didn't mean it the way you took it. I said *you'd* get used to being here with no one but grown people in the house, and that your feeling lonely wouldn't last long. Not with Fergie and Andrew around."

Cory gave a sigh of relief.

"Well, am I glad — I really am! You know, I had the biggest, longest dream I've ever had in my whole life. And it was so *real*, but all I can remember now is something about unicorns —" At her own words her eyes went round with alarm and her hand flew to her neck. But there it was — she still had it. "Something about a chess set. I wish I could remember —"

"Would you like me to teach you to play chess?" Uncle Dirk was standing at the door as if he was about to go.

"What?" cried Fergie, who'd been busy straightening the room. "Ye mean teach a wee speug like that to play *chess?*"

"But I can play, Fergie. What's a speug?"

"A wee sparrow."

Both Mrs. Van Heusen and Uncle Dirk were smiling.

"I mean really play chess, Cory — not the way children do, but with skill. Would you like that?"

"*Would* I! Could we right now?"

"I'm afraid not. I only came up to get some blueprints from the workroom — I have an appointment in twenty minutes. But we'll play some night soon when you're chipper again."

"I'm really chipper now," said Cory after he had gone, but both Fergie and Mrs. Van Heusen thought she should stay in bed until the next morning, and meanwhile Fergie said she would bring up some chicken broth. "And toast too? I'm starved — Fergie, before you go could I have *The Five Little Peppers?* I haven't read it for years. It was right here on the bedside table, but it's gone."

Fergie got it from where she had put it back on the shelf, then she fluffed up Cory's pillow and put two more behind it so that she could sit up and read. But as she and Mrs. Van Heusen turned to go, she stopped suddenly.

"I forgot to tell ye — Peter and his Explorers were here. I told them ye were sick, so they said they'd come back another time, and Peter sent up his best regards. I really thought they had such nice manners that I gave them gingerbread and glasses of milk. The gingerbread had just come out of the oven, and they did seem to enjoy it — so much that I had to make two more pans! They'll come, darling," said Fergie as she followed Mrs. Van Heusen into the hall. "Don't ye worry about that."

Cory opened her book, but she could hardly read for making up a story about how it would be when Peter and the Explorers came back again.

Seven

HOWEVER, they did not come back.

Cory thought surely she would hear them laughing and shouting outside, perhaps calling her from the trail along the cliffs, or that Peter at least would come knocking at the back door. The second day after she was well again, she took the cliff trail over to his house, but no one was home, not even Mrs. Hawthorne, and though Cory went down on the beach where she had met Laurel Woodford, and stayed there for two hours hunting for shells and colored stones, there was no sign of the Explorers.

On another morning when she went back to the beach, she looked up and saw them in the Hawthornes' garden. Eagerly she waved, and Peter lifted his hand in return, but then they all turned away and did not come down the stairs to the beach. Cory somehow couldn't bring herself to tell Fergie about this. What she did want was to remind her about the mince pie and inviting Peter over to dinner, but Fergie right now was rushed and red-faced, immersed in a thorough spring housecleaning in preparation for a large dinner party Mrs. Van Heusen was planning to give.

Now there were only three days left before school would begin again. At least if I could go with Peter and the rest, thought Cory, then I'd get to know the Explorers that way.

"But I doubt very much if the school would take you for the two months left before summer vacation," said Mrs. Van Heusen when Cory questioned her at lunchtime. "And then, I understood that Stephanie would be sending for you in a week or so."

"But would I *have* to go, Grandmother?" pressed Cory. If only she could go to school *and* stay all summer! Yet somehow, in the face of Mrs. Van Heusen's silence, she could not bring herself to ask for this as well.

After a little: "I don't know, Cory. I really don't know what my plans are right now."

And there would not have been an atom of use in saying anything more.

On this late, still afternoon, warm in the sun but already growing cold in the shadows, Cory was exploring at the back of Tarnhelm up behind the rose garden.

From where she stood, she could look down through the pines and see how beautifully Andrew had laid it all out, the giant pansies thick in their borders around the roses, and behind the pansies, on all sides, ranks of pink and white carnations, tulips, daffodils, hyacinths, snow-drops and crocuses, pale golden columbine, deep blue delphiniums, as well as Mrs. Van Heusen's favorites, whose scent Cory could catch even from up here — the bronze, velvet-petaled wallflowers.

> "Wallflowers, wallflowers, growing up so high,
> All you young ladies were all meant to die —"

Cory hummed under her breath the snatch of song Mrs. Van Heusen remembered from when she was Cory's age, and went on burrowing her way through a jungle of wild lilac that shed its minute lavender-gray blooms across her back and shoulders as she climbed.

> "Wallflowers, wallflowers, growing up so —"

She stopped, for all at once the wild lilac gave way to a hedge of mock orange covered with fragrant white nubs of flowers, exactly the kind of hedge that bordered the drive down below. And presently, having squeezed between two bushes, Cory did in fact come out onto what was plainly a continuation of the lower drive whose main sweep led to the garage. But this part of it was lost in the rustling pine wood, lost and neglected and overgrown.

The asphalt here was cracked and buckled, weeds were growing through it in clumps, and the whole of it was scattered with drifts of needles as if it had not been used in years. Cory followed it through the trees up to a gate in a fence so thickly covered with an old honeysuckle vine that the fence itself was scarcely visible. The iron gate was intertwined with long tendrils, but Cory could tell from the marks on the driveway that the gate must have been pulled back and forth at one time or another.

Wonderingly, she opened it. There were no houses higher on the headland; the only people living anywhere near the Van Heusens were the Hawthornes over on the other side. Mystified, Cory stole on up the road, followed around curve after curve, feeling as if she should be stepping with the silence of an Indian. Birds watched her, talking back and forth among themselves and darting overhead from branch to branch. Squirrels scolded, "Nya-a-ah, nya-a-ah, nya-a-a-ah!"— furious that their private wood should be trespassed. And then, coming around a final bend, she saw that she had reached the top.

Opening out before her stretched a broad green

meadow surrounded by tall pines and thick with lush, knee-high wild oats across which a little wind chased itself, leaving a silvery trail where blades turned, now here, now there, as though someone unseen were running. On every side stood stacks of lumber of all thicknesses and widths, weathered to gray. And when Cory went forward she discovered down in the grass what seemed to be part of a foundation, and then — exploring further — saw that here, high above the sea, hidden from any eyes that might look up from Tarnhelm, a house was to have been built that had gone no further than its cement base.

Now all at once she stared up, and there was Peter. He grinned at her and came over.

"Me'n the Explorers've known about this place for ages. Of course, other times after the grass gets all dried up, you can see the foundation better and then it's easy to have different rooms and do all sorts of things. Sometimes we have a fort, or a mansion —"

"But who does it belong to? Who was going to build a house?"

"Well, the Van Heusens, I guess. Haven't they said anything? We always stay quiet so they won't hear. Boy, I bet your uncle'd chase us. We always put a lookout down the road so's we can be warned — two short whistles and a long one —"

"Why, I bet he wouldn't even care. It doesn't look as if they're ever going to finish. What'll we do, Peter — make up something?"

"Nope," said Peter, turning away, indifferent. "It wouldn't be any fun with only two. You've got to have a whole bunch to be lots of different people."

"Well — what, then? What would *you* like to do?"

Peter looked up and studied her, and there was a glint in his eye.

"I'll tell you what I'd like to do — I'd like to find out if that's a real tower or not — the one sticking up near the back of Tarnhelm."

"I'll bet it is, and I'll bet there's a stairway leading up from Uncle Dirk's workroom."

They raced across the meadow to the road and, filled for some mysterious reason with smothered laughter, spied out from the shrubbery to be certain no enemy was lurking. Then, huddled down, they crept the long way round the garden to the side door beneath Cory's bedroom windows and tiptoed in.

"This is silly," whispered Cory. "Fergie wouldn't care —"

From the front hall they could hear her out in the kitchen bashing pans; then, still silent, they sneaked up the front stairs. Cory led the way along the upper hall and couldn't resist stopping to show Peter her four-poster bed and the fireplace.

"Cri-kee-ee!" he exclaimed. "A real fireplace in your bedroom — do you *light* it? What a funny bed, like a house. I didn't know people still had them. That's what kings and queens used to have."

"I know," said Cory. When she opened the door of Uncle Dirk's workroom —

"Boy," said Peter, "what a swell place — two big, huge tables to spread out on. That's what I'd like to have, and all those millions and millions of drawers. I bet that's where he keeps his plans. What's this over here? Oh, darkroom," and he went in. "Everything for developing pictures." Cory could hear him opening and closing boxes and drawers, and presently something smashed when he dropped it on the floor. But already she had crossed to a door on the far side, opened it, and come into a little hall leading to another door at the end. However, what she had been hunting for were these stairs mounting on her left.

"Here they are, Peter — the tower stairs," she called, her voice high with excitement. Then, "What was that you broke?"

The darkroom door slammed and he was after her.

"Golly, what a house! I wonder where that door there goes to? Let's find out when we come down again."

At the top of the sunlit, dusty stairs, they came into an exceedingly small, dusty, hot tower room that smelled strongly of mice and with windows all the way around — windows that couldn't have been washed in years, perhaps ever — set deep in the stones. There were window seats built under them, and the first thing that struck Cory's eye was a piece of wood, half-carved, and by its size and the shape of it, and by the beginnings of details already cut, she knew it was to have been a mask. But of whom? She would take it down and ask Uncle Dirk. Now, what was Peter doing? He was smoothing out some sheets of paper, curled and yellowed, that he had found on the floor, but in a moment tossed them aside.

"Poetry," he said in disgust, and Cory picked them up and saw the shapes of verses, lines of different lengths in groups all scribbled and written over and some crossed out entirely. Uncle Dirk trying to write poetry, or the person he had been carving? Cory folded up the papers and kept them, to be examined later.

Meanwhile Peter had knelt on the seat to have a good long stare out of the windows. "Gee whillikers," he breathed, "what a place to play sentries and spies and crusaders and —"

"Would the Explorers like it up here, Peter?"

"Would they *ever!*"

"Well, get them, then — and I'll tell Fergie, and maybe she'll make gingerbread and you can all stay for dinner —"

"Honest?" Peter's green eyes widened. "O.K.! But I couldn't get them now — maybe tomorrow —"

"Well, let's go ask Fergie to make *us* some gingerbread and *you* can stay for dinner. Come on —" Again excitement rose in Cory's throat. Happiness swelled in her chest like a big, almost bursting balloon. Never in her life had she asked anybody to stay for dinner.

They rattled downstairs, snatched open the workroom door and — there was Uncle Dirk standing staring at them. She grinned at him and slowly brought up the mask and put it over her face as she had done with the one of Stephanie. But there were no eyeholes and she could not see his expression.

"Where did you get it?"

She took the mask away.

"Why, up in the tower, Uncle Dirk — it was —"

"Give it to me, please. And those papers?" He took the mask and put it on the drafting table beside him, and he unfolded the papers, swept them with a single glance, folded them up again and put them in his pocket. He did not speak for a moment, and then, "I would appreciate it, Cory," he said in a quiet voice that sent a ragged sharpness through her because she knew at once that he was only just managing to hold back his anger, "I would appreciate it if you and your friends would respect our privacy." By "our" she knew deeply that he meant his and his mother's, the family's, the *real* family's, made up in this house of just those two. And she was the outsider — and she had not respected their privacy.

"Excuse *me!*" said Peter, and in one swoop he was past Uncle Dirk, out of the door and down the hall. "Sorry about that glass —" he called back.

"Oh but Peter!" cried Cory, darting after him. "Peter — don't forget — don't forget about the Explorers —"

He was lunging down the stairs two at a time when she got to the top, and he turned and looked up, and he made a horrible face and shrugged up his shoulders and spread his hands as if to say, "*See* — what'd I tell you — your *uncle* — !" In another second the front door banged behind him like a cannon shot.

Cory sat down on the top step and crossed her arms and put her head down. How *could* everything change so fast? How *could* it? And when Uncle Dirk passed her a few minutes later —

"Uncle Dirk, I'm sorry — I never thought —" but couldn't trust herself to say any more.

"Forget it," he said lightly, without turning, and went on down. But in the lower hall he paused. "Go and clean up the pieces of that beaker you and Peter broke in the darkroom, Cory. And don't go in there again, and especially don't ever leave broken glass lying around." Then the front door closed for the second time, and the whole house was as still as if there weren't a soul in it.

It was an enormous relief to Cory to know that Grandmother and Uncle Dirk were eating out that evening and that she was to have dinner all cozy with Fergie and Andrew.

> *"Yin, twa, three —*
> *Ma granny cotched a flea,*
> *She r-roasted it an' toasted it*
> *An' tuk it tae her-r tea — !"*

sang Andrew, sitting down at the table and giving his napkin a fling to unfold it. Cory watched him, warmed a little by his gaiety. Roasting and toasting a flea! Then he held up his glass of milk and waited, smiling at her, for her to hold up her own glass and clink it.

"Here's tae us," he said. "Wha's like us!"

It was their usual toast, and Cory loved it. Here's to us — who's like us!

"Such a dreadful, self-satisfied thing to say," laughed Fergie.

"It's no dreadfu'," retorted Andrew. "It's just tr-rue. After all, there isn't anybody *just* like us."

Cory silently started to eat, but with no appetite, and

114

presently she felt Fergie's sharp eye upon her and Fergie's hand was laid on her arm.

"What is it, darling? Ye're not hungry at all, and that's very unlike ye. Surely ye're not feeling badly because the Explorers haven't been round? But they don't know ye, ye see, and they'll be having their own affairs, so ye'll just have to be patient until ye can go to their school and get acquainted gradually. I thought about the mince pie, but ye wouldn't want to bribe Peter."

"No," said Cory. "Anyway, it wouldn't be any use —" and then she told them all that had happened, every single thing. "And now Peter'll *never* come back. He'll tell the Explorers how mad Uncle Dirk was and they'll never come either — never — never — let alone let me into the club."

"Och, r-rubbish!" exclaimed Andrew. "Ye take things far too seriously, lassie."

"Yes, ye do, Cory dear," agreed Fergie. "Peter'll likely have forgotten the whole thing by tomorrow. But why should Mr. Dur-rk get so upset over an old mask and a few bits of paper, I wonder? If they meant so much to him, why d'ye suppose he's left them up in the tower all this time? But darling, ye must remember that Mr. Dur-rk and yer granny are very *private*. They cannot abide nebby people or gossips — like that Mrs. Smallwood, for instance."

Nebby. That meant nosy and prying.

"Aye," said Andrew, and chuckled, apparently relishing his memories. "I saw her downtown today and she wanted to know how Cory was making out with the Van Heusens. She'd like sneaking tidbits — she's always trying to get r-round me in the market."

"There's something she wants to know," said Fergie. "Something she wants to ask, or something she wants to tell. And it delights me to put her off —"

"I don't think she likes Uncle Dirk or Grandmother," said Cory, remembering her drive with the Smallwoods along the highway.

"Then she'll just have to nur-rse her dislike in her bosom," said Fergie, her eyes sparkling, "for I'll tell her nothing, and listen to nothing. Yer granny and yer Uncle Dur-rk are odd at times, but they're fine, good people and I'll listen to nothing against them. If we have our difficulties, we'll just keep them to ourselves inside the family." Fergie got up with their emptied plates. "And now would ye like a dab of ice cream on yer plum tart, Cory dear?"

Cory, having confessed her unhappiness and disappointment, was feeling much better.

"Two dabs, please, Fergie. Big ones, if you don't mind."

Eight

THERE was no telling about Uncle Dirk, Cory decided.

When, with a knot of anxiety in her stomach, she came into the breakfast room the next morning, girding herself to face him, to deal with whatever mood he might be in, he simply glanced up and smiled at her and said good morning just as if nothing out of the ordinary had happened. And Mrs. Van Heusen didn't say a word about getting into mischief and breaking things or going into other people's rooms and taking what didn't belong to you.

And when Cory had finished and asked to be excused, Uncle Dirk looked at her standing there beside her chair.

"Cory, you remember when I came in to see you after you'd been sick and promised I'd teach you how to play chess?"

117

"Yes," said Cory, "I remember —"

"Well, how would you like to begin this evening?"

She gazed at him in astonishment.

"Oh, Uncle Dirk! *Could* we?"

"Why not? Right after dinner, then. It's a date."

"But I'm probably not very good, not compared to you," said Cory that evening from where she waited at the chess table with its light and dark checkered squares inlaid in the top. It had been put at a little distance from the fire and within viewing distance of Mrs. Van Heusen, who sat with her book in a large wing chair near the hearth. With the drawn curtains, the firelight red on the paneled walls, the grand piano gleaming rich and dark in a far corner, comfortable chairs scattered about, as well as a great many books and magazines, and the wind brushing branches against the windows, Cory decided that this was her idea of a perfect room.

"Well, I don't expect you to be an expert," said Uncle Dirk, who was searching through a cabinet for his chess set. "When I see what you can do, we can go on from there. Fergie," he called. "Fergie, what did you do with my —"

"It's there, Mr. Dur-rk." And Fergie came straight in and got the set from the cabinet on the other side of the arch. Then she said, "Tchk!" and while Uncle Dirk and Cory began setting out the pieces, she brushed up the bits Andrew had left when he brought in more logs.

"Yer Uncle Dur-rk carved those pieces, and he made the table, too," she said, slipping her hand along Cory's shoulders as she passed by on the way out, then paused to watch as the ranks of light and dark men were lined up in battle formation. First, in the very back rows, one at each end, came the rooks, or castles. Then, going in toward the center, the knights, the bishops, and the kings and queens in the middle, with the little pawns facing each other across the board in the rows in front, protecting their masters. The pieces were very plain, but had been sandpapered and waxed and rubbed until it was a pleasure to handle them. "Can ye play at all, darling?"

"Oh, yes," said Cory. "I play with Mr. Tuttlefield, who lives along the hall from us at home. I go in after school lots of times. He was the one who taught me."

"Mr. Tuttlefield!" exclaimed Uncle Dirk, as if he enjoyed the name. He held out both hands, one closed over a dark piece and the other over a light. Cory chose the light one and so it was her first move. She slid out a pawn. "Don't people have marvelous names?" Uncle Dirk went on, moving out one of *his* pawns. "I had a Mr. Trotworthy for a teacher when I was a boy. What opening are you going to use, Cory?"

"I don't know what you'd call it." Now she moved out a bishop.

"I see — not any definite opening. But you ought to learn some of them. You can't be called a chess player without that. Well, we'll go along with this for the first game just to see how you do." He moved one of his own bishops out.

"And do you remember that friend I used to have, Dirk?" asked Mrs. Van Heusen, folding her hands across her book. "Her name was Trixie Gosliner." Uncle Dirk smiled to himself, leaning back in his chair, and Cory moved her queen out, clear over to the outside of the board in the castle's file, but Uncle Dirk wasn't looking. He seemed to be trying to remember something.

"There was someone you told me about, Fergie —"

"I knew a woman in Scotland when I was little," said Fergie, "whose name was Effie Limpetlaw."

"Limpetlaw! Limpetlaw! That's it!" cried Uncle Dirk. "I remember you said she —" Then he saw Cory's queen and he shook his head, frowning. "Now, why would you move your queen out like that so early in the game when you haven't even castled? It's a wasted move. I expect Mr. Tuttlefield told you about castling . . . the king moving two spaces to the right and the castle two spaces to the left all in one move."

"Yes, he told me."

Now Uncle Dirk pushed out another pawn. "Limpetlaw!" he repeated, shaking his head again. "I think that's a wonderful name. I used to make lists of specially good names when I was a boy —" and then he stopped suddenly with his arm out. He saw what Cory had done and he stared at the board, flabbergasted.

"Checkmate," said Cory softly.

Her heart was pounding, her hands were cold, and one of them was holding her silver unicorn. It was ridiculous, but this trick she had played was something Mr. Tuttlefield had taught her, and it was called Scholar's Mate. She had never dreamed it would work on Uncle Dirk. What she had done was to quietly move up her queen and take his pawn in front of the bishop on his king's side. Thus she had closed right in on his king. And the king couldn't fight back by taking Cory's queen, because there was her bishop lying in wait directly behind her queen to checkmate his king if need be. No other piece of Uncle Dirk's could capture her queen in revenge to save the king, and his king was penned up with no least loophole of escape.

Uncle Dirk was finished. The game was over and Cory had won.

"Why, I can't *believe* it!" cried Mrs. Van Heusen. She tossed her book aside and came over to stare down at the board as Uncle Dirk was doing. Then she put back her head and laughed and laughed. "And you

121

were going to teach her to play with skill, Dirk — not the way children do!"

Cory saw Uncle Dirk's face flush red, and at that moment Cory felt Fergie's hand lift from her shoulder as she went quickly away.

"I never did understand a thing about that game," she said.

Oh, thought Cory, and now her hands were colder than ever (cold as puddocks, Fergie would have said — a puddock was a frog), what a fool I've been — I should never have done it. Uncle Dirk and I were

122

friends again, and now I've ruined everything and he'll
never want to play chess with me any more. Why did I
have to be so smart right on top of yesterday?

"Uncle Dirk wasn't watching," she said in a muffled
voice.

"All the same you checkmated him — you *did* it!"

But why did Grandmother have to rub it in?

"Yes," said Uncle Dirk all at once, "you did it, Cory,
and I've no excuse, except that I wasn't watching —
going an about people's names — and I wasn't thinking." Cory gazed up in relieved astonishment. "You're

123

a spalpeen, that's what you are, catching me like that."
He wasn't angry! Far from it, he was grinning at her.
"Come on, let's have another go."

And so they did have another go.

The game took a long time, and there was no laughing and chatting now. All was silent except for the wind outside, the almost subterranean thud of the surf, the whispering flicker of the fire and the soft crash of one log falling against another. The clock ticked to itself on the mantle and there came the sound of a page turning now and then as Mrs. Van Heusen read. But she looked up often to give the board a shrewd, appraising glance. Then Cory would catch that gray gaze resting on her own face, as if Mrs. Van Heusen was trying to determine what could be going on in Cory's mind. And every once in a while Uncle Dirk would murmur, "Good, Cory, *good!* Ex-cellent move!"

And when the game was over and Cory was finally driven into a position where there was no way out and Uncle Dirk said in a low voice, as she had done, "Checkmate," he looked over at his mother.

"I can hardly believe it. She's a natural, that's what she is. Either that, or this Mr. Tuttlefield is a genius of a teacher. I haven't enjoyed a game so much for a long, long time. She really *sees!*"

"*Do* you, Cory?" asked Mrs. Van Heusen, leaning forward, her eyes alight with interest. "*Do* you see more than just one move ahead? Do you see patterns on the board?"

"I don't know," said Cory, overwhelmed by their praise. "I try to plan ahead — and I try to figure out what the other person's up to. I'm not just sure *what* I do, though sometimes I can see quite a few moves on both sides. But my end game's no good, Mr. Tuttlefield says."

"Not as good as the rest," said Uncle Dirk. "That's what you've got to work on. All the same, it's extraordinary — and at your age! You're a witch, Cory — an imp, a troll — you put a hex on me the minute you sat down."

"That's what Andrew said the first night I was here, that left-handed people are bewitched." Absently Cory reached out and picked up a knight in the shape of a horse's head, its neck curved, its chin pressed down against its throat and its ears tilted forward. The knights in most chess sets are like this; but there were knights she had seen once in another form, not too different, but magically so. Carved of wood, they had been, too — and they had felt like this; your hand wanted to caress their silky gloss. Yes, she remembered. It had been in her dream.

"The knights should be in the shape of unicorns," she said, almost to herself, "rearing up on their hind legs with their forefeet pawing the air, but with no riders on their backs. That would be too much, because unicorns are magical enough just by themselves. And the bishops should be real bishops with miters on their heads, and the castles real castle towers. And the kings and queens should have crowns on their heads and be dressed in a medieval way. I saw a chess set like that. You remember I told you, Uncle Dirk? It was in a dream I had, and there was a big dark room with moonlight coming through the windows. I wondered if, after I left, the pieces would go on living."

Uncle Dirk was staring at her with the strangest, most unreadable expression on his face.

"*Go on living?*"

"Yes," said Cory. "Acting out their lives. The unicorns would have had enough magic in them to make the whole set come alive, so I couldn't put them back. It would have been so crowded and undignified for them to be all jumbled together in a box, and if I left them out, then things could happen. There could be stories, with the pawns running errands and taking messages and spying in the ranks of the other army, and there would be counsels and intrigue, and the kings and queens quarreling and then coming together again." She had been staring right through Uncle Dirk, seeing the elegant pieces almost as vividly as if she were in the midst of her dream again in that vast, shadowed room with, under the windows, those cabinets full of mysterious objects she had not quite been able to make out. "They had faces, I think — the kings and queens — with eyes and lips and little fine noses. They seemed so real to me, I felt I had only to turn around and the story would go on right where it had left off when I discovered them —" Her voice trailed away, and then she came to and saw Uncle Dirk and Mrs. Van Heusen with their eyes fixed upon one another, but what this meant Cory could not fathom.

"You say it was a dream, Cory?" Uncle Dirk turned back to her. "You're perfectly certain it was a dream?" He sounded almost accusing, and this too she could not understand. Her eyes widened in puzzlement.

"Why, yes, it was a dream. It was when I was sick, when I had the fever, and you and Grandmother and Fergie came in when I finally woke up. I told you —"

"What else did you dream? Was that all — just the big room?"

"I think so. No — I remember now. There was music, sad, slow music, and the moon kept getting smaller and smaller, and then it would grow huge, and then get little again. And Stephanie was there, on the beach, only I couldn't see her. And she told me I didn't have the re — the requirements to be adopted. She sounded as if she didn't really like me at all —"

"Oh, what nonsense, Cory!" exclaimed Mrs. Van Heusen in that flat, definite way she had. "Absolute nonsense!"

"But it was a curious dream," said Uncle Dirk. "I think Andrew's right, Cory. You *are* bewitched."

But why am I? Cory wanted to ask, utterly bewildered. In what way? However, she could not ask, for something seemed to be over between her and Uncle Dirk, at least for now. He was not unfriendly. It wasn't that. But, gathering up the chess pieces, putting them back all orderly in their box, he seemed to Cory to have withdrawn so that she couldn't easily ask, as she would have done only five or ten minutes ago, any question that came into her head. Another of his moods seemed to have come down over him. And now he took the box and put it back where Fergie had gotten it from. Then —

"Goodnight, everybody," he said and went out, and Cory knew he was going up to bed to read, or to his workroom, perhaps, where he would begin sketching out the plans for a new house.

"Is there something the matter, Grandmother?"

"No, of course not —"

"Did Uncle Dirk think I was fibbing to him, that it wasn't really a dream?"

"Why would you ask that?" Mrs. Van Heusen's eyes searched her face.

"I don't know — I just had that feeling."

"But it *was* a dream."

"Oh, yes. And I remember I felt sick and feverish and as if I didn't know where I was — at least in the dark room with the chess set in it."

There was a small silence. Cory was still at the chess table, but now she got up and went and sat by Mrs. Van Heusen on a footstool, leaning against the chair with her arms around her knees, staring at the fire. "What kind of name is Dirk, Grandmother?"

"It's Scottish. A dirk is the dagger of a Highlander. Perhaps I should never have given him that name — I don't know what possessed me, because there've been times when he *has* been a kind of dirk — sharp, sudden, turning now this way, now that." Cory looked up at the patrician face with its fine nose and clear forehead and dark eyes, and saw that Mrs. Van Heusen was looking away as if she'd forgotten Cory, as if she were talking to herself. "Sometimes the blade is silvery and warm, at others — cool. And you never know — you're never certain — and yet, there is great kindness there, great goodness, with the blade turning inward mostly."

"What do you mean, Grandmother?"

"I mean that Dirk has hurt himself far more than he has ever hurt others — except one. Yes, except one."

"And Van Heusen?"

"That's Austrian. My husband was Austrian and I

Scottish. A fine mixture, isn't it?" She smiled, as if re-membering scenes out of the past. "But surely Steph-anie's told you all this —"

"No, she hasn't. I always mean to ask her so many things, but when she gets back from one of her tours, there's so much to tell me about herself and everything that happened. Anyway, you're Scottish, too, like Fer-gie and Andrew."

"Yes, which is why I was so happy to find them. They seemed like a breath from my childhood, and when I'm depressed or unhappy, I have only to hear Andrew singing in the garden one of the Old Country songs, or go out into the kitchen and talk to Fergie, or perhaps she comes in to me, and we have tea and hot buttered scones and we reminisce about our childhoods and I'm all right again. I have grown very fond of Fergie and Andrew in the short time they've been here."

I too! cried Cory in silence, with passionate longing. In the short time *I've* been here — I too! Of Fergie and Andrew, of you when you're like this, of Uncle Dirk when we're happy together, playing chess in this room with the fire going and the wind outside and the sea thudding on the beach. Of my room that used to be Stephanie's. If only I didn't ever have to go away! If only — *if only* — I belonged!

Again they sat together in silence, and presently Cory felt a hand stroke back her hair, absently, lightly, and she stayed as she was, quite still, so that the mood between them should not be broken.

"Oh, I wish I were a doo' —" began Mrs. Van Heusen softly (and Cory knew that doo' meant dove, because this was a poem Andrew had said to her once):

> *Oh, I wish I were a doo'*
> *An' I'd flee awa' the noo,*
> *Wi' ma neb to the north*
> *An' ma wings beatin' steady.*
> *An' I wouldna rest a fit*
> *Till at gloamin' I would sit*
> *Wi' ither neebor doo's*
> *On the lums o' Balgeddy.*

Neb meant nose, and fit meant foot but:
"What's lums, Grandmother?"
"Chimneys," said Mrs. Van Heusen.

Nine

FERGIE and Cory had been hanging out clothes back of the kitchen garden in the hedged-in drying area, and now they had gone to the cliff wall to look out over the ocean. It was another perfect day of pouring sun, blue sea and crystal air. A freshet of wind blew against them, brisk and pure. The tide was far out, so that the enormous boulders at the foot of the cliff stood up dry, with tide-pools in their hollows winking in the sunlight. When the waves came in, then drew back, there was a rough, grating sound as the smaller rocks and pebbles were tumbled and dragged together in the swift, out-going surf. Cory heard shouts and, peering down, spied Peter and the Explorers swarming round the farthest headland toward the inlet beyond, a thing they could never have done at high tide. Her heart lifted, and all at once, as if he had felt her eyes on him, Peter looked up, and when she waved he waved back.

"There now," urged Fergie, "go on! Go on over to Peter's house, an' ye can meet them when they get there."

Cory hesitated. She saw the rest of them look up at her and then, without stopping, continue on and disappear beyond the headland. "No," she said. She wanted to go. How she wanted to! But the sinking in her stomach said no. She could just imagine the others saying to Peter, "Do we *have* to have her? What did you want to go and wave for? We could've pretended we didn't see her." "No," said Cory.

"Och, ye're a wee puddock, always hopping off by yer lone. Ye've too much pride entirely."

"Why do you always have to be so sure people want you?" Stephanie would say crossly. "Why won't you ever take a chance?"

But, actually, thank goodness, she didn't have to take chances when Stephanie got home. "Pick up my things for me, will you, Cory? Make my bed for me, will you? There's a dear. And you can help me unpack — I don't want that Mrs. Seed poking her nose around in my room — and just iron these few things for me, will you? I can't stand the way Mrs. Seed does them." It was fun helping Stephanie unpack, seeing the new clothes she'd bought, the jewelry and dresses and nightgowns, the gossamer underthings, and the purses and gloves and shoes and belts, smelling richly of the finest leather. All the same — "Haven't you been *any-where?* No wonder you're so pale and peaked-looking, staying stuffed up in this place every day after school. You look awful. Why don't you and Mrs. Seed go to the park?" If there was one thing Cory would have hated more than anything else, it would have been going to the park with Mrs. Seed.

And another time —

"When I was your age," said Stephanie firmly, "it would never have occurred to me to wonder whether people wanted me or not. I just went and played. In fact, I was the one who always thought up things for everybody else to do."

"Well, but I'm not you when you were my age," Cory had pointed out with equal firmness. "In fact, I'm prob'ly just the exact opposite."

Now Cory looked out across the sea and she could feel a heavy lump in the pit of her stomach. It was an old feeling — she knew it well: disappointment in herself, which always, at first, seemed to be disappointment in happenings.

"Fergie," she said suddenly, "sing me the 'Skye Boat Song.' "

And so Fergie did, letting out her whole voice, because there was no one there but the two of them.

The next morning, which was the last Friday of

134

Easter vacation before school began again, when they were having breakfast in the kitchen — Fergie and Andrew and Cory — the phone rang. There was a telephone on the table in the front hall, one in the upper hall, and one out here in the kitchen on the Welsh dresser. And when Fergie answered, she turned with a sparkle in her eye and held out the receiver to Cory.

"A gentleman friend," she announced impressively.

Cory could scarcely believe it — it was Peter! And he was going on a hike and wondered if she wanted to come along.

"Oh, Fergie, could I?"

"I don't see why in the wur-rld not, as long as ye're careful —"

"And don't go scrummaging round any places ye shouldn't," added Andrew.

"I can go, Peter."

"Now don't bolt yer breakfast, darling. If Peter gets here ahead of time, he'll just have to wait."

But Peter did not have to wait. He appeared at the back door at the end of precisely ten minutes, just as he'd told Cory he would, and his auburn hair was roughed up from the wind as if he'd been running and his greeny-blue eyes gave off sparks of energy. He had a large package under one arm —

"A skirt this weaving woman made for Mom — but

135

it's too big." They'd have to go along the highway, he said, and then up a mountain road in a canyon to where the weaver lived. It would take about an hour there and another coming back — "so we'll be here again about noon, Fergie."

"Well, ye must have lunch with us, then," said Fergie.

As if he knew exactly what he was doing, without hesitating a moment to figure anything out, Peter set off through the rose garden and led the way through the wild lilac hedge and up the deserted drive to the honeysuckle-covered gate.

"But why *this* way, Peter?"

"Shortcut," said Peter briefly, and having closed the gate behind them, hustled on up through the still woods. "No use going down the other road, because the weaver lives way over beyond the Smallwoods in the redwood forest."

A surge of happiness swept through Cory. A weaver in a forest! It was perfect — and now not a drop of day-before-yesterday's bitter disappointment over Uncle Dirk and the tower and Peter not staying to dinner, after all, was left. Peter was cutting across the meadow in the direction of the highway and then they were running downhill through the woods toward the high stone wall that bordered Tarnhelm property.

"I never expected to see you again after Uncle Dirk got mad at us the other day," panted Cory.

"Oh, he's not so bad, I guess. I saw him down at the entrance this morning and he asked me if I was going up to Tarnhelm by any chance, and I said I was busy and had to go on an errand up to the canyon. So then he said he thought maybe you'd like to go if I wouldn't mind taking you along."

They had arrived at the wall, and now Peter reached up and put his package on top, but Cory stayed where she was, staring down at the ground. Her eyes shone, her mouth straightened, and her chin drew up.

"And here I thought it was your idea!" She looked up at him. "But you didn't *have* to ask me. You didn't *have* to take me along just because Uncle Dirk said you should." She turned and began scrambling back up the hill. She *hated* pity. She was lonesome, with nobody to play with, so he'd taken pity on her and it hadn't even been his idea.

"Don't be a nut," called out Peter, exasperated. "I don't mind having company —"

"Don't mind — don't mind —" stormed Cory. "I thought you wanted —"

"O.K., then — if you're going to act like an infant," said Peter. Cory, glancing back, saw him grasp the top of the wall with both hands and pull himself up. Strad-

137

dling it, he glanced up at her on the side of the hill a little above him. "No wonder you have a hard time making friends —"

"I never said I did," retorted Cory furiously.

"But I could tell," said Peter, remorseless. "You're the kind you have to get down on your knees and beg 'Please come — *please* come —' " mimicked Peter cruelly.

She wasn't! But what had Fergie said? She had too much pride. And it was true, it *was* hard for her to make friends. But how had Peter known! What else did he know about her from what she'd told him that she hadn't meant to tell?

"If you want to be an Explorer you have to hike," he said. "And this is a good hike. Only with all that huffing and puffing, you'd never make it anyhow." He gave her one last disgusted look, dropped down out of sight on the other side, and a second later the package disappeared too.

"Peter!" yelled Cory. "Peter — wait a minute —"

Sometimes they chattered and sometimes they were silent, going along contentedly at a steady, spring-footed pace in their sneakers, first near the highway, well away from the edge of it, then whipping across when there weren't any cars in sight and beginning another of Peter's shortcuts.

Up they went across broad, rolling fields furred in juicy grass as though the pleats and folds of the hills, mounting in one gradual rise after another, wore a thick green pelt that would turn golden as the summer months came on. Scattered across the hills were vast flings of yellow buttercups and deeper yellow mustard, pale yellow and lavender wild stock, orange poppies and monkey flower, purple lupin — veils of lupin as though a giant had breathed out his great purple breath — and patches of red Indian paintbrush. Enormous clouds swept over, trailing majestic shadow. Above the children's heads white-bellied swallows darted on slender, blade-shaped wings, soaring, pausing like held breaths in mid-air to catch insects. Meadow larks sent forth their clear, sweet calls. In fenced-in pastures, dotted with clumps of oaks, brown-and-white cows grazed and a sprinkling of black ones.

"Herefords, those brown-and-white ones are," said Peter knowingly, "and the black ones are Black Angus from Scotland."

They passed the Smallwoods' little house, perfectly silent in its own grove of pines at the end of the road that led up from the highway. And beyond this, higher up, they came to the wall of a forest, thick and deep with varying shades from slightly yellow-green through to the rich green of the redwoods that holds a hint of blue in the shadows. Cory saw the pointed crowns, the lifted tips of the pine branches and the layered, heavy fronds of the redwoods slowly rising and swaying like dancers' arms, lifting and swaying and dipping.

It had gotten hot in the sun and she could feel her cheeks scarlet from the long way they had come, but it was cool in the shade. She could hear the wind ranging the forest, and thought how there are three sounds that are almost alike — the wind in the trees, the rushing of a river, and far-off tumbling of the sea. All three of them would be a part of her for the rest of her life.

Through the trunks of the pines and redwoods, she looked out over the Pacific, far, far below.

"Peter, what were you and the others doing yesterday?" she asked suddenly before she could stop herself. "I mean, when Fergie and I looked over and saw you at the foot of the cliff. Anything special?"

He did not answer at once; he seemed to be thinking. Now they were going up again, their footfalls padded on thick, springy beds of needles, and all was quiet in the forest except for the nickering of a squirrel or the harsh call of a jay or a crow.

"We have caverns, the Explorers and me," he answered finally, just when Cory had begun to think he didn't intend revealing anything. "And we have treasures we keep secret in a certain place. I found another treasure the other day."

"Down there?"

"Yes. It's a box, a carved box —"

"Uncle Dirk used to carve."

"But this is real old. It must have been around for centuries. Anyway, it's our private treasure."

"Peter, could I see it? Could I see the caves?"

"Sometime. We'll take you down sometime."

"But you said you'd bring the Explorers to Tarn-helm sometime, and you never did. I don't believe you."

"All right," said Peter lightly, not at all in a mean or unfriendly way, "don't then."

He was infuriating, he was so independent, and yet somehow — and why, she did not know — this was one of the things she liked best in him.

"There it is," he said, pointing upward. "That's the weaver's house. You'll like her. She's different from most people."

They had come into a canyon, along the bottom of which wound a narrow road. And as Cory looked up, through shade cut across with brilliant, slanting shafts of gold, she saw in a pool of sunlight a small white house that seemed hung as if by magic against a green so deep as to be almost black. It dazzled the eye in the dark forest.

"What is the weaver's name?" asked Cory.

"Laurel Woodford," answered Peter.

Laurel opened the door and stood there staring at Cory.

"It's the girl on the beach!" She said it low, her voice sounding as if she could not believe it. She held the door wide and Peter went in and Cory slowly followed. She noticed that Laurel had on that same pull-over sweater, the one the exact color of her eyes . . . gray-blue. "I'd been thinking about you this very minute. And now, suddenly, you're here!"

"What were you thinking?" asked Cory, strangely joyous. She, too, had thought about Laurel; she'd wondered often, as she played on the cliffs and looked down

beyond Peter's house at the curving beach, if they would ever meet again. Once or twice she had gone to the beach alone, and when it grew misty she was sure Laurel would come, as if Laurel were some enchanted being who could appear only at a certain time. But she never had. "What were you thinking?"

"That you should have heard from your — from Stephanie by now. Have you? I've so often wondered."

"No," said Cory. "I go down to the mailbox at the highway every morning, but the answer hasn't come yet. Stephanie's not very good at writing."

"Where's your mother now?" asked Peter.

"In France, I guess."

"Can she speak French?"

"Oh, yes — and Spanish, too."

"Is she like a movie star?"

"Yes, like that — or, at least, she's a stage actress."

"Is it exciting?"

"Well," said Cory, "it is, sometimes, I suppose — anyway, for Stephanie. But this is better. This is much, *much* better."

The room had been all light, Cory told Fergie and Andrew when she got home that evening. That is, it was filled with light, but not bright, not glaring.

"Luminous," said Fergie.

Yes, said Cory, that was it — and it seemed airy because there were so many windows and so much space, so that it was like an eagle's nest, high up above everything in the treetops, with a huge view of the ocean and the whole forest below.

"But don't you get lonesome way up here by yourself?" Peter had demanded.

"Not very," said Laurel. "I have so much to do."

Her loom stood at one end of the room, with a smaller one nearby, and she showed Cory and Peter how she shot the threaded shuttle back and forth between the taut strands of the warp, which she had already set up. It looked so easy when Laurel did it, but when Cory tried, the shuttle went whirling away and the thread got all tangled. Laurel had woven the draperies at the windows; she'd made the rugs on the floor — "They were silky," said Cory that evening, "and all of the most beautiful soft colors." When she and Peter and Laurel had sat down to lunch, you could tell the mats were hand-woven too.

"I was glad you called me about lunch," said Fergie.

"Well, but of course you were expecting us back. We had waffles with lots of butter and syrup, and bacon, and then fruit and cake for dessert. Afterwards, Laurel put the pineapple and melon rinds and some other leftovers outside the window, and the raccoons came and held the rinds up in their hands. There was hardly a scrap left when they were through and the melon rinds were paper-thin, so that you could practically see through them. She says the deer come down, and sometimes wildcats — or is it mountain lions?"

"Oh, *not* mountain lions!" exclaimed Fergie.

"Well, now," said Andrew, "I've heard that back in the farther ranges of hills there are mountain lions. But of course not here, not so near the coast. Wildcats — yes. Bobcats, they are, or lynx, some people call them. The ones with the legs too long for their bodies and little short, broad tails."

"The ones wi' the tufts in their ears?" cried Fergie. "*Good*-ness, I wouldn't be wanting beasts like that round my house —"

145

"Ho!" said Andrew. "Bobcats never hurt anybody. They just vanish off in the trees. I've seen 'em once or twice. Homely things they are."

Anyway, Cory went on, after lunch Laurel took out an old photograph album to show them pictures of her when she was Juliet in the high school Shakespearean play. She was thinner then, with bobbed hair — and of course it was long now, done up. But still, she'd looked herself, and there was one picture of her in the balcony scene, leaning over toward Romeo, and another of her when she was down in the tomb with her arms crossed on her chest and a big candle at her head and one at her feet. She said that when Romeo came and found her, supposedly dead, then stabbed himself, and she woke up and kissed him, he kissed her back as loud as could be. And as he was *really* supposed to be dead, the whole audience shouted with laughter and teased her about it for days afterwards.

Now Cory stopped, remembering something.

"You know, that was funny. Peter and I kept turning over the pages, looking at Laurel and her friends in high school, but all at once she took the album and closed it up. She said that as she got older, she got thinner and thinner and looked so homely she didn't want us to see — but I didn't think she was homely."

"Well, I can understand," said Fergie. "I never like

people to see snapshots of me, I take such a dreadful picture."

"Och, ye don't either," exclaimed Andrew. "Silly woman!"

"Just before we went," continued Cory, "she played something on the piano I wish I knew the name of."

"Hum it," said Fergie. "P'raps we'll know what it is."

"But I can't — I tried to remember it on the way back, and I can't make it come right. I keep thinking about it. I can hear it in my head and I'm sure I've heard it somewhere before. I like it so much, I wish I could remember it."

Ten

ON THE night of Mrs. Van Heusen's big dinner party, Fergie had in a girl to help her with the food and all the other innumerable preparations. However, well ahead of time, she had baked two large mince pies.

"Oh, Fergie, *could* I ask Peter to dinner?"

"Yes, of course, darling, as long as ye behave and stay out from underfoot."

But mince pie wasn't to be the main dessert. "In Scotland," said Fergie, "the great company dessert is trifle." And the way you made it, Cory found, was this: you cut up a pound cake into slices and spread the slices with raspberry jam, then you arranged the slices three layers deep in an enormous cut-glass bowl and you soaked the layers with sherry "— or berry juice, p'raps," said Fergie, "if yer family doesn't approve of wine." After this you poured on plenty of cooled custard, spread whipped cream on top, and decorated the

148

whole concoction with walnuts and maraschino cherries and little round macaroons, and with pieces of candied angelica cut in the shape of leaves. Cory gave a moan of pleasure as Fergie slipped the bowl into the refrigerator.

Peter could hardly wait for the mince pie, but "You haven't seen anything!" said Cory fervently, and when he beheld the trifle, he couldn't resist, and had to have both it and the pie. Fergie thought he would be sick for sure, but he wasn't — not even beginning to be.

Later on, after everyone went into the living room, Cory was asked in to be introduced, and Peter too. And it was then that Andrew was called upon to sing. At first he wouldn't be budged when the children were sent to get him.

"Och, I'd just have to change into my other clothes, an' it'd be a ter-*ri*-fic nuisance."

But nobody cared about his clothes, they sent back word, they didn't care two cents how he looked. They just wanted him to sing.

So in he came, just as he was, and Fergie, as well, to play for him. And he sang "Annie Laurie" and "The Far Coolins" and "The Wee Cooper o' Fyfe" and "Wrap Me in Your Plaidie, Laddie" and "Flow Gently, Sweet Afton," as first one, then another of the guests asked for some special favorite.

Andrew did not sing to impress. He had no tricks, he

did not move his hands. Indeed, he did not move at all, but stood there looking away, quite still, perfectly relaxed, with his arms down in front of him and his hands clasped together. He sang what was in his heart, softly and tenderly, with absolute simplicity and naturalness, and you could have listened to him for as long as he cared to go on.

As he sang "Flow Gently, Sweet Afton," two things happened. Cory saw Uncle Dirk get up and go out, and then she happened to look over at Fergie, playing, and saw her watching Andrew. And in that moment she realized for the first time in her life that older people, people Andrew's and Fergie's ages, can care very deeply for one another after being married for thirty or thirty-five years. She had never thought about this before. People that old were just married, that was all, and they probably jogged along out of habit and it couldn't be very exciting, she might have felt if it had ever occurred to her, because everything would be quite ordinary. They would be so used to one another.

But not so — *not so!* She knew this now to the depths of her being.

Then she thought of Uncle Dirk. Why wasn't he married and having happiness like theirs, feeling everything she saw so plainly in Fergie's face as Fergie listened to her husband singing the songs they both loved while her eyes rested on his face? Uncle Dirk was so handsome (at least *I* think he is, thought Cory) that it was mysterious indeed if he'd never even been engaged.

After Peter's father came and took him home, Cory had to go to bed. But when she was in her room and about to close the door, she happened to glance over and noticed the light under Uncle Dirk's workroom door, and then Mrs. Van Heusen came hurrying upstairs and along the hall.

"You must come down, Dirk," Cory heard her say in a low, urgent voice.

"I don't feel like it, Mother — and I've got to get this plan finished. Now please leave me alone."

"You *haven't* got to get it finished. I know you haven't. And these people are your guests, too — I think it's disgraceful, going off like that and just leaving them. It's not right, Dirk. You're the host."

So at last, silently, he got up and came out and went off with her, and all was still on the upper floor. Cory got into bed and lay there thinking, staring into the dark. Fergie was right. Uncle Dirk *was* a strange man, but not the way Peter had thought he was in the beginning, not mean, not ever — in the least. Maybe he was just unhappy about something and it showed sometimes. Maybe there wasn't anything he could do about it.

Eleven

WHEN Andrew and Cory set off for Carmel in the station wagon on Monday morning to do the marketing, the mail hadn't come.

"But my letter from Stephanie will be here today, Andrew," said Cory as they drove off.

"Now how would ye know that?"

"Well, I'm not sure how, but I just do. I have a prickling feeling in my stomach that her letter will be in the mailbox for me when we get back."

"Second sight, is it? But of course — ye're cawry-fisted! Ye're bewitched!"

Now they were spinning along past Point Lobos and then past the long crescent-shaped beach just beyond it, across from the monastery; and there, going down toward the waves, with the skirts of their black habits and the wings of their white headdresses fluttering in the wind, went a little group of sisters from the Villa Angelica, out for a walk.

"Where's the shopping list, Andrew? Where do we go first? And can I stop by the library?"

"Of course ye can. Let's see now, here's the list. Table water biscuits, Fergie's got, and puffed cracknels and digestive biscuits. Digestive biscuits! Tasteless abominations! To go with yer granny's fruit and cheese, no doubt."

"Oh, and spinach, it says, Andrew," groaned Cory. "Four bunches, fresh, *un*packaged."

"Spinach!" cried Andrew. "I canna abide the stuff. An' ye should just see the trouble Fergie has to go to. Fur-rst she poots the whole mess in a gr-reat vat o' water. Then she washes an' washes an' washes it till ye' think there'd be nothin' left. Then she gets out a huge pawt she keeps clear at the very back o' the cupboard, an' she looks at each leaf an' she shakes it off an' poots it in the pawt. Then she dumps out the dur-rty water, poots in clean, poots all that spinach back in, and then she washes an' washes an' washes *again*. Then she studies each leaf again, an' shakes it all off — and *then* she cooks it. An' when it's done, it's *far-r-r* wur-rse than it ever was r-raw, an' it's *still* fit fer nothin' but hor-rses."

They drove straight down Ocean Avenue toward the sea, past all the little shops crowded with people even this early in the morning, even at this time of year, people in tweeds as if for cold weather, people in linens and sport shirts as if for summer vacation, and young ones with long golden-brown legs in very short shorts. And sometimes the sun was out, warm and sparkling, and sometimes it was in, with a hint of fog out at sea. But nobody minded whether it was warm or cold, and nobody minded the little nipping, crystal-edged wind that blew in under the tall Monterey pines growing down the center of the street. Healthy-looking old ladies and gentlemen strode along in thick jackets and flat, sensible shoes and with walking sticks on their way to the post office to get the mail. Everybody was looking, buying, laughing, stopping to visit, darting across, getting out of cars, getting into cars, and the traffic was thick and constant.

"I love it here, Andrew!"

"Aye, but there's no dar-rned place to park what with all these confounded tourists. They don't even wait till summer any more. Now here's the library. I'll be back in three quarters of an hour, honking for ye, an' ye're to be out here, because I don't want to have to go round and round."

"I'll be here, Andrew."

Inside the library, down a few steps on the left in the children's room, Cory hesitated. What did she want? Oh, yes — *The Story of the Amulet*. She found it and settled at one of the tables and in seemingly no time at all came to with a start and stared at the clock. What a relief! She still had fifteen minutes, but now where had she put Mrs. Van Heusen's library card? A few moments later she was sitting outside on one of the stone seats at the edge of the sidewalk waiting for Andrew, lost in her book again, when all at once there came a voice right beside her.

"Well, well, well, well — I see you reached the house safe and sound by the look of you. Move over, dearie —"

Cory gazed up and there, beaming from under the familiar pot-shaped, flower-laden, dusty old hat, was Mrs. Smallwood in her black silk coat and all her beads and bangles and her purse big enough to hold a flannel nightgown *and* slippers *and* a brush and comb. Reluctantly, Cory moved over.

"Oh, hello, Mrs. Smallwood," she said faintly, not closing her book.

"A little fatter and not so peaked and washed-out-looking — that's good — that's good!" The old lady moved close, putting her face down near Cory's, her pale little eyes intent. Cory unconsciously moved back. "Tell me, dearie," she said in a low voice, speaking very clearly, "how are you making out? Any difficulties, eh?"

"Why, no — no difficulties, Mrs. Smallwood. I don't know what you —"

"Oh, *you* know! Not very used to children, are they? Cool and distant was always my experience." Mrs. Smallwood's mouth drew up and her eyes darkened. "Always was," she repeated bitterly. "Always tried to be civil and friendly, but they wouldn't return it."

"But, of course, it's different with me," protested Cory. "After all, they're my family —"

"So they are," said Mrs. Smallwood. "So they are. That big house — nice on the inside, is it? Nice, thick carpets and drapes and everything? And say, do they have any help besides those two Scottish people? I sh'ld think they'd need maids for a big place like that. Though lots of times, places like that, they look so big and elegant on the outside and all, and when you get in 'em — 'tisn't anything. Ordinary as the back of my hand with not a lick of style."

"Well, I like it," said Cory, rebellious, moving back and back until she was squeezed into the corner of the stone seat. "I think it's —"

But Mrs. Smallwood wasn't listening. She was remembering.

"A spoiled, snobbish, indifferent young cub, yer uncle was in those days. Oh, I remember him driving around here as if he owned the place, and once I was standing right up there on the corner — that corner there — and it had been raining and I was waiting to cross. And you know what he did? He came along in his new sport car and went whizzing round the corner and splashed mud all over me, head to foot, and I had a brand-new dress and coat on, the most beautiful I'd ever owned — that coat was — and they were both ruined, absolutely ruined, and I was on my way to a friend's house for lunch. Well, I went home and cried —"

"Oh, but Mrs. Smallwood, surely Uncle Dirk didn't mean —"

"No, of course not. He never meant to do any of the careless, rude things he *did* do, but they happened all the same. Cold and arrogant, he was then, just like his mother — never stopped to think, not once —"

Cory sat in miserable silence, wondering what she could possibly say to Mrs. Smallwood, who was looking off at nothing as if she were going over every slight and injury she had ever suffered at the hands of the oblivious Van Heusens. Probably that was the worst part, that Uncle Dirk and Grandmother hadn't even been aware.

"Cory!" shouted Andrew. He honked vigorously. "Come on — hurry — I'm holding up the traffic —"

"I've got to go, Mrs. Smallwood. Goodbye — goodbye —"

Away went Cory, her book clutched under her arm, and hopped into the car and slammed the door behind her.

"Thank goodness, Andrew! Oh, thank goodness! It was getting worse and worse." Then she looked up at him. "But do you know what? I feel sorry for Mrs. Smallwood."

When they got out on the highway, Andrew began singing at the top of his voice out of sheer good spirits and in a wonderful, swinging rhythm:

> *"Oh, the bonny wee barra's mine —*
> *It doesna belang to O'Hara,*
> *For the fly wee jock*
> *Has stuck to ma rock,*
> *An' I'm going tae stick tae his barra!"*

"What does that mean, Andrew?
"That? Why that means,

> *"Oh, the fine little wheelbarrow's mine —*
> *It doesn't belong to O'Hara,*
> *For the sly little man*
> *Has stuck to my candy,*
> *And I'm going to stick to his barrow.*

Much better the first time, wasn't it?"

They sang and sang all the way home, first one and then another of Andrew's silly songs, and Cory's heart grew light. But the minute they got beyond Point Lobos, a strange thing happened. Without any apparent conscious thoughts or fears to begin it, her heart sank, then painfully quickened its beating, her stomach went heavy and hollow, and at the same time her hands became cold.

Andrew drew up at the mailbox, Cory opened the door and in another moment was pulling out two handfuls of mail, which she tossed onto the front seat of the car. And there — just as she knew it would be — was an envelope with Stephanie's big, familiar scrawl. Siliently Andrew gathered up all the other mail and silently sat while Cory tore open the envelope with trembling fingers, spread out two thin sheets, and began to read. Then her hands, with the two pages, dropped to her lap.

"Oh, Andrew —" she said in a sick voice.

"But what is it, lassie — what is it?"

" 'Dear Cory: I was terribly —' " here Cory stopped to get control of her voice as she started to read — " 'I was terribly upset to receive your letter in London, and you know I simply *cannot* be upset when I'm on tour because it affects everything I do. To me, it was the utmost thoughtlessness of Dirk and Mother to have told you everything as they did — this was for me to do, and I would have done it in my own good time and in the way I wanted. Anyway, Cory, I simply *cannot* go into it now, about adopting you and all that, because it would take ages and ages to explain everything and I haven't either the time or the energy at present —I am *very* tired! I can't *tell* you how all this has upset me. Dirk and Mother should have known how unhappy it would make me to have you write about it, and it seems to me it was quite selfish of all of you.

" 'So now, on to happier things. Cory, I can't *wait* to get back — well, no, that's not the honest truth because I'm having a perfectly marvelous time — a magnificent tour — everything is an enormous success with full houses every night and the matinees too, both in London and here in Paris! And so I shall have *lots* of money when I get back, and Cory dear — we're going to get a place in the country, and this time we'll keep it. Think of that! You know how I adore the country. Oh, I know I tried it before and it didn't work, but that's because I ran out of funds, but it'll work now. I know it will. And you won't mind changing schools again, will you?

" 'What's more, a dear friend of mine is flying to Japan and she wants me to go along and stay there for a week or so at the home of her people in Kobe, so I'll be coming across the Pacific and landing in San Francisco and will fly from there to Monterey to pick you up in about a month. I'll let you know the exact date later. All my love — Stephanie.' "

"It didn't wur-rk, eh?" said Andrew. "The place in the country?"

"No," said Cory. "It didn't."

When Andrew and Cory came in the back door, loaded with bags of groceries, Mrs. Van Heusen was sitting at the table in the kitchen with Fergie.

"But I *do* remember, Fergie," she was saying. "And the *Marchioness of Breadalbane*, that fat, stumpy little boat that used to go waddling along with two paddle wheels going thump, thump, thump, one on each side, down the Clyde, away into the Firth headed for the islands — The Wee Combrie, we always used to go to —"

"Oh, *yes*," cried Fergie, "and there'd be a bit of an orchestra on the upper deck made up of a harp and a violin and a concertina — my, but it was lovely! Hel-*lo*, darlings. Here, set the bags on the floor — not on the table, Andrew — and Cory can lay out the silver for lunch while I put the groceries away. Yer grandmother wants to eat out here with us." But suddenly her gaze fastened on Cory's face. "Why, whatever's the matter?"

Silently Cory handed her letter to Fergie, who took one look and gave it to Mrs. Van Heusen. And when Mrs. Van Heusen had finished reading, she sat quiet for a moment, and Cory saw that two little red spots had come into her usually ivory cheeks.

"Stephanie always was the center of her own universe." She handed the letter to Fergie, who glanced at Cory and started to read.

"But a place in the country, darling," said Fergie uncertainly. "That would be very nice, wouldn't it?"

This was too much. Cory flung her head down on her arms on the table and burst into tears.

"No, it *wouldn't* be nice, Fergie! It *wouldn't*! Because we won't stay, and it'll all be for nothing —"

"The truth is, Fergie," said Mrs. Van Heusen, "Stephanie does *not* simply adore the country —"

"She hates it," sobbed Cory. "She said so last time — she hates it and everything about it. She can't stand the quiet, and not seeing people, and not being able to go to plays and movies, and being so far from the shops and all her friends —"

"But maybe now —" persisted Fergie.

"Oh, Fergie," said Mrs. Van Heusen wearily, "it's no use. It will only mean the child will have to change schools for the fifth or sixth time, they'll live in the country for the summer and fall, and then just as Cory gets into the new school — back they'll go to New York again. It's as plain as can be: Stephanie has once more been carried away by the elegance of riding to hounds, the idea of her own horses, the home woods and perhaps a dairy and an orchard and all the rest of it. I've heard it a dozen times — a beautiful old house in Connecticut, out in the hills —" Mrs. Van Heusen waved her hand and then sat there staring at Cory.

Silence, while Cory's sobs continued briefly, subsided, then stopped altogether.

"What a strange, difficult family we are," mused Mrs. Van Heusen. "Hard on one another, I mean, in spite of affection."

"Was Stephanie difficult when she was a child, Grandmother?"

"Very, very difficult. Stubborn, headstrong —"

"Yes, that's what she's told me herself."

"Worse than me, Stephanie?" she'd asked Stephanie once.

"Oh, *you!*" cried Stephanie in amused scorn, as if Cory were nothing but a mouse, a soft, yielding kitten by comparison.

But if I ever really wanted anything, Cory thought now, if I ever really wanted anything with my whole heart and soul, maybe Stephanie would be surprised. I wouldn't be a mouse or a kitten. I'd fight for it with every bit of myself. *Well, then, why didn't she?* She wanted something now more than she'd ever wanted anything in her entire life: and that was to belong somewhere with a family that she could call hers, who would adopt her, a family like Grandmother and Uncle Dirk and Fergie and Andrew who really stayed home and who would be there all the time. That was what she wanted. Only it was hard to fight for something that took so many other people's decisions. It wasn't as if she could just struggle hard toward one thing that depended on herself alone. She could have done that, she was sure of it. But this was different. All the same —

"Grandmother," she said, and her heart started up again the way it had when she and Andrew had been driving toward the mailbox, "Grandmother, do you suppose — do you think maybe I could live here with you and Uncle Dirk? I mean, do you think I could stay?"

Mrs. Van Heusen turned and looked at Cory. She sat without moving for quite a few seconds while she continued this serious, studying look.

"But Cory," she said at last, "that would depend upon Stephanie. You're her child — I can't just suddenly tell her I've taken it into my head to keep you. Obviously, she has other plans —"

"Oh, but Grandmother, I don't want to go back. I don't want to be taken care of by lady-helps — it's so hard to get the right ones, and Maureen McQueeny's the only good one we ever had — she was wonderful! — but she didn't stay."

"But don't you love Stephanie? I believe she loves

you. Haven't you felt like her child all these years? You didn't *know* she hadn't adopted you. What difference does the piece of paper make, Cory?"

Cory was silent, turning this over in her mind. But it wasn't just that she hadn't actually been adopted. That wasn't really it — at least that wasn't all. Now that she came to think of it, it had always been as if Stephanie were her older sister, flashing in and out of Cory's existence like a bright — what? Like a dragonfly, shimmering blue and green and bronze. When Stephanie was there, it was exciting (at least, in a way), with the phone going, friends flocking in, the talk and laughter and the spoiling (Cory stayed up late, ate what she shouldn't, shared in the fringes of gossip and complicated tittle-tattle). But sooner or later the lady-help's nerves frayed. She blew up and Stephanie blew up; then Stephanie's nerves frayed and she blew up at Cory. Then made up with her, was briefly contrite; they went on shopping expeditions; Cory was treated to lunch at the very best restaurants, was taken to whatever plays and movies were fit for her and to some that weren't. Then everything tapered off again; the first edge of homecoming wore thin. Next it was all over and Stephanie had settled into her usual New York life of being out every evening, away every weekend, until once more there came another tour.

"I don't think Stephanie would really mind if I stayed. We see so little of each other, and I feel as if I belong here. With lady-helps you can't ever belong."

Fergie's eyes sparked and suddenly she slapped her hand down on the table. "That's it — *that's it!*" she said as if she were enormously angry, then got up all at once, went over to the sink, drummed water deafeningly into the kettle and rattled it across the stove.

But Mrs. Van Heusen's face closed.

"Cory," she said, "I have had my day of bringing up young ones, the worry and responsibility, and I feel I'm past all that now. I feel I have a right to my peace and quiet."

"But Grandmother, you could *have* your peace and quiet. I wouldn't have to be a worry and a re — or at least, not a worry —"

"No child can help being a worry," said Mrs. Van Heusen sharply. "Heaven knows Dirk and Stephanie were constantly that — I never knew what was coming next." Then she looked at Cory again and must have seen the intensity in her eyes, for her own suddenly slid off sideways as if to avoid what she saw. "But of course it would have to be up to Stephanie. She likes to have you there to come back to —"

"The child has her uses, no doubt," observed Fergie tartly, whipping shut one of the cupboards.

"— and you are hers," continued Mrs. Van Heusen.

Silence, while Andrew stuffed his pipe and Fergie continued to make small crashes in the background. "That has always to be remembered, that you are hers and that she's taken care of you all these years. But we'll see, Cory. I'll think about it, *that* I promise you. Now do finish setting the table so that we can have lunch."

Twelve

WHEN school began again, it was decided by Mrs. Van Heusen that because Stephanie would be coming to get Cory before the middle of June, it was no use asking the school people if they would take her for just a few weeks.

"Even though I *might* be staying *after* Stephanie comes to get me?" reminded Cory with hope.

"Don't harp, dear," said Mrs. Van Heusen. "I'm turning it all over in my mind as I promised you I would, but you must let me decide undisturbed. Otherwise it makes me impatient."

It was a suspenseful time.

"Terribly suspenseful," said Cory to Fergie, "because there are two things suspending and both so awfully important . . . whether I can stay and why Stephanie hasn't ever adopted me. One waiting until

Grandmother makes up her mind, and the other waiting until Stephanie gets here. Sometimes, if I think about it a lot, it makes my stomach tight."

"Then ye must try not to think about it," said Fergie.

Meanwhile, things kept happening, and one of them made Cory feel that perhaps Uncle Dirk wouldn't have minded her staying.

She had been studying the masks in the hall, and when Fergie called them in to dinner, Uncle Dirk came along and, putting his arm around her shoulders, walked with her to the breakfast room, where they always ate when there were no guests.

"Why don't you carve any more, Uncle Dirk?"

Now they were at the table, and Grandmother sat there watching her son with rather a waiting look, Cory thought, as if she would be interested in what he had to say. But he only shrugged.

"You certainly couldn't earn a living at it," he said.

"Oh, did you use to carve to earn a living?"

Uncle Dirk smiled.

"Well, not really. I just loved doing it." He paused and studied his own hand on the table. His fingers flexed together as though he was thinking of skill and strength and the feel of the wood taking shape beneath his hand. "I stopped about seven years ago and took up architecture —"

"But how could you just *stop*, Uncle Dirk? Stephanie said she'd die if she couldn't act. Didn't your fingers want to carve — don't they now?"

Uncle Dirk studied her, his eyes serious and searching.

"How do you know about an artist's fingers wanting to do their work?"

Perhaps she and Stephanie had talked about it; she couldn't remember. "But I should think it would be sad," she said slowly, "for a real artist to suddenly decide to stop painting or a pianist to stop playing. I should think their fingers would want to begin again. I should think yours would."

Uncle Dirk did not answer.

"I expect Stephanie told her," said Mrs. Van Heusen. "Or she heard Stephanie's friends talking."

"Perhaps," said Uncle Dirk. "All the same, I'd like to take her to see the wood carvings at the museum in San Francisco. Would you like to go, Cory? And we could see the aquarium and the natural history museum and have lunch somewhere. Perhaps we could go on a weekday as soon as I've finished the house I'm working on —"

"But I only have another three weeks, Uncle Dirk. Do you think you would be through before then? Or perhaps it doesn't matter if —" and she turned to Mrs. Van Heusen, meaning that maybe there wasn't any need to be urgent if she would not be going back to New York with Stephanie after all. But Mrs. Van Heusen only smiled vaguely and unansweringly, as if there were nothing being considered, nothing of the slightest importance hanging in mid-air to be decided by her single yes or no.

"Well, we'll see," said Uncle Dirk, in such a way that Cory felt certain he hadn't been told she had asked to stay. "If it's at all possible, we'll do it."

But now, without warning, everything turned out very badly.

How, Cory asked herself afterwards, are you ever to know what fate has in store for you so that you can try to watch as you go along and act accordingly? Sometimes, as in the case of Stephanie's letter, she had feelings about what was going to happen. But now she was taken completely unaware, and in the beginning it had all seemed so happy. Peter phoned to ask if she would like to come over Saturday noon for a weenie roast. The Explorers would be there, he said, and he thought this would be a good chance for her to meet them.

"But will they mind my coming, Fergie? I mean, maybe they're expecting it to be just an Explorer party. I'll bet Peter's mother *made* him phone because he was over here to dinner."

At this, Fergie looked stern.

"Now, I don't want to hear any such remarks as that," she said. "I don't want to hear any fears or hesitations, or ifs or ands or buts. I want you to go and enjoy yourself."

So Cory went. She was excited, uncertain and, despite Fergie, fearful. When she got to Peter's house, she would have gone up the stone steps to the garden, where she could hear laughter and voices, with one hand around her unicorn, except that she was carefully carrying a box with nine meringues in it that were not

to be jolted and therefore perhaps crushed or broken. There were seven meringues for the party and one each for Mr. and Mrs. Hawthorne. She heard a girl burst out laughing — would that be Bip or Maxie? And would they pretend she wasn't there? Would they ignore her so as to keep it an Explorer party? What would they be like?

Augie, whose real name was Augustus, was tall and bean-pole thin and he had a quick grin, but he didn't say much, and his freckles were uncountable. Roddy was square and chunky and solid, with brown eyes so dark as to be almost black that narrowed to slits in his round face when he laughed. And he often laughed as if he was enjoying some private joke. Kev was a little button of a boy, who reminded Cory of a mosquito with his quick dartings here and there. Bip, whose real name was Barbara, was almost as tall as Augie. She had smooth, straight blond hair pulled right back and tied as if she wanted it out of the way, and she had no smiles — at least not yet. She watched Cory out of quiet, studying brown eyes. Only Maxie, Kev's sister, curly-headed and as light and bird-boned as he was, came over at once with a welcoming face.

"What's that box for? This isn't a birthday party —"

Peter turned from where he was stirring up coals in a cone-shaped metal container on legs. He gave her a quick, teasing look.

"Well, come on, silly — don't just stand there. You won't get any eats that way —"

"What's in the box?" demanded Roddy. He had three weenies on a stick and was turning them slowly, with rapt attention, over the coals. Cory opened the box and showed the smooth, crisp, cream-colored shapes.

"They're meringues," she said. "You take off the tops and put ice cream and strawberries inside. Then you put the tops back on and put strawberries all over them with a blob of whipped cream on top."

174

"You *do?* Crickey!" said Roddy solemnly.

Everybody's head bent over to look and they all seemed to be picturing this mouth-watering operation. Then Mrs. Hawthorne came out to say hello to Cory and to rescue the meringues, and the Explorers went back to roasting weenies. There were also, arrayed on a trestle table, a large bowl of potato salad, a plate of deviled eggs, another of pickles and tomatoes, a bowl of baked beans and a basket of buttered buns.

"— but don't keep *eating* so much, Rod," said Peter, "or you won't have any room for dessert."

"Who cares?" said Augie. "Then we can have his."

"When we go on a hike," said Maxie to Cory, who had been given a long stick with two weenies stuck on it, and making room for her in the circle around the barbecue, "we just take a sandwich and an apple, but Roddy takes a paper bag just *stuffed* with sandwiches and cake and a bar of candy and a banana, and afterwards he's still hungry."

"You know what?" said Peter. "Cory could teach us how to play chess — I mean really play. Her uncle told my dad she's a whiz, maybe sort of a genius —"

"No!" said Cory quickly, darting a glance at Bip out of the corner of her eye. "No, I'm not, Peter —"

"Well, awfully good for your age, anyway. And you could start to teach us. After all, we ought to have intellectual pursuits, too."

"What're they?" demanded Kev, wiping his mouth off with his arm and spreading mustard right across his face. "Intellekshul whatever you said?"

"Well, games like chess. That's sort of an exploring. We could have tournaments whenever it's raining too hard to go out, and Cory could be the Chess Master of the club — I mean, if we voted her in after a while."

Cory's heart beat hard and her face reddened. She looked down, frowning, at the plate in her lap and endured the short, waiting silence that followed.

"Peter, don't *glug* so when you drink," said Bip suddenly. "You always glug."

"But I can't help it," said Peter. "It's my Adam's apple. I've always noticed boys drink louder than girls —"

Everybody laughed and went on chattering, and presently Mrs. Hawthorne called out to Peter to come and help her bring the plates with the dessert piled on them, and after that there was a long, blissful space with no sounds but the waves collapsing on the sand and spoons clicking on plates. Roddy winced a little when he first broke into his meringue. After a bit —

"It only lasted about two or three minutes," he said regretfully when he had finished, "but it was absolutely great while it did." He went on scraping up crumbs and faint traces of pink.

176

Later they went down on the beach and Maxie said, "Shall we show her our caves?"

"Oh, *yes!*" said Cory. Her cheeks were scarlet from running, for the afternoon had grown gray and damp and cold. A thin mist, not so thick as fog, had crept in over the sea, invading the whole coast so that the headlands were only vaguely to be seen. The Hawthorne house on its wooded perch seemed to have retreated. There was not a soul on the beach but the seven children, so that they might have been all alone in the world except for an occasional gull or cormorant, wheeling and lighting, silently rising, emitting sharp, single cries. "Please show me your caves. Peter told me about them and that you have treasure —"

"Why did you?" demanded Bip, staring accusingly at Peter.

"I'm president," returned Peter calmly. "I can do it if I judge a person's trustworthy. But I didn't tell *where* —"

"Oh, come on," said Maxie. "Why shouldn't she see them?"

Kev and Augie and Rod were already climbing up among the rocks below the Hawthornes' house to get to the path that led around toward the gorge. *This* is the path, thought Cory happily, scrambling after Maxie and Bip, *this* is the path they were heading for when

Fergie and I looked down that day, and I waved to Peter and saw them disappear. And now I'm here, and I'm going with them to the caves, and they're not going to disappear, at least not from me.

You had to cross the bottom of the gorge over to the Tarnhelm side, and then go on for a bit. And when you first went in, there seemed to be only one cave, with a firm, upward-sloping sand floor. But when you went clear to the back, it was like rooms under the cliffs, hundreds of feet beneath Tarnhelm property, one cave leading to another through narrow passages, and the children's voices sounded ghostly and hollow and echoing as they called out to one another.

As they went in, Cory saw the line of surf lapping up, lapping up round the foot of the boulders outside the cave's mouth. And at that instant a strange bronze sun broke through the winding mists, shone startlingly as if in a stage-play on the gray and silver sea, and lighted up the inside of the cave. And when they went into the other caves, how mysterious the children looked to one another in that queer light, that eerie reflection. Mysterious sounded the hollow booming of the sea, muffled came the rough rattling of the stones caught in the undertow, the whisper and sigh of spent breakers.

"Shall we play Spanish Discoverers, or Pirate Smugglers, or Escaped Settlers?" asked Kev.

They played all three, one after the other, and Cory

could tell they'd played each story time and again, changing them a little, perhaps, as they went along, adding on, embroidering, and now she found herself suggesting. putting her imaginings in too. Nobody said so, but Cory thought that maybe they felt she was a good maker-upper, because they accepted her new end to Pirate Smugglers just as if one of them had offered it.

But all at once, in a single second, the inner caves, where they had been acting out Escaped Settlers, grew dark. The sun had been smothered at last in the thickening mist, or had been drowned in the sea. Now it was evening, and —

"What's that?" cried Cory. She listened. She heard water slapping as if in an enclosed space, and in a second had darted out to the main cave and saw that the farthest reach of the tide had come up beyond the entrance. Unbelieving, standing rigid for an instant while the meaning of this swept over her, she went then and peered out, and saw that the strip of beach where they had come was now cut off entirely, that the foot of the nearest boulder was completely covered, and that they could not possibly any longer make their way round the headland to the gorge beyond. She turned to stare at Peter and Augie and Kev and Rod and Bip and Maxie, sick at her stomach with shock and horror.

"Well," said Peter fatefully, "that's that," and he

and the rest of them turned away and went back into the cave.

"*We're caught* —" Cory tried to call out to them, following after, but no words came. She flung her arm across her mouth so that they wouldn't guess that sobs of terror were bursting up in her chest and that her chin was shaking.

"Everybody hang on to somebody else," said Peter.

No one answered, and they all, except Bip and Augie, went on ahead, intently discussing something among themselves. And then Cory understood — they would not admit fright; they would not show terror and weakness; they were Explorers, not babies. Therefore she did not let herself put out her hand and cling to Bip, who was just in front of her, but only tried to keep close and to swallow the questions that kept wanting to struggle up: what would they do if they could not find another way out? How long would they have to wait before the tide went back? And the final, most chilling question of all: if the caves had been eaten out by the sea, how far would the tide come in now?

"Will we —?" began Cory. "Will we be —?" Trapped, she tried to say, or drowned, but could not, or would not.

"Will we be what?" inquired Bip. She and Augie turned and stared at her, and it was strange, but in that dim light their eyes seemed to Cory to be cold and their faces were flat and inimical. And yet why should they be?

"Nothing," she said. "I stumbled."

Blackness closed around them. There were breathings, feet slipped, knees and shins were bruised, ankles turned, there were exclamations of pain, warnings, smothered remarks, though what these were about Cory could not hear because at regular intervals the caverns were filled to echoing with the bursting crash of tons of sea water falling into the outer cave.

"Will it —?" asked Cory finally in a shaken voice, "will the tide —?" but could not force herself to finish, "— come all the way in?"

They went on in silence, feeling their way, putting out their arms to protect themselves from the brutal knife-edges of the rocks that pressed in on them. If only we could see just a little, thought Cory, just a little. She took hold of her unicorn for a moment and felt a wave of sick panic rise in her chest, surge up in her throat. But she would not let it out in a cry. She would not let them know that she had never wanted to sob so bitterly and despairingly in her whole life. And it was Fergie she thought about most —

"Fergie!" she wanted to shout. "Fergie, Fergie — help us!"

Then, in a little, when it did not seem possible that they could keep going back and back any longer, Cory thought she spied, not a speck of light, but a vaguely spreading grayness. Now she could make out the shape of someone's head far in front of her — and then, like shadows, the heads of the others. And at last —

"But it's the gorge!" burst out Cory, dumfounded. "Why, it's the gorge —" an outcry that was lost in a confusion of shouting.

There was a patch of sky and trees beyond the rough outline of a break in the surrounding darkness. It grew brighter and brighter, and when Cory caught up with the rest of them, they were looking out from this rocky gap in the Tarnhelm side of the gorge over at the Hawthornes' house high on the opposite side. Laughing and calling to one another, they scrambled down into the bouldery bottom of the gorge and, when they had landed safe, Cory slid down after them and then danced up and down in excited triumph — but noticed suddenly that they were all concentrating on her, so that she stopped dancing, her mouth open, her eyes going from one to another in puzzled questioning.

"Why, you didn't *know!*" cried Maxie. "You thought —" and she stared at Cory, and now Bip and Augie burst out laughing and, for two breaths, as Cory stood facing those two, she was filled with hatred and hot fury.

"*You knew* I didn't know!" she exploded at them, trying to break through that wall of derision. "*You knew* —" but they only laughed and laughed as if they were having fits, and Cory all at once went for Bip, striking out blindly and wildly, but Bip, cool and strong and lithe, flipped her aside and then her laughter tailed off into gasps, and "I don't care," shouted Cory, swallowing her rage, "I don't care — we're safe." She flopped down, humiliated to the core of her soul, and hid her face against her doubled-up knees.

"It looks as if it turned out to be a sort of initiation," said Peter seriously. "Initiations are supposed to be tough, but we never thought about you not knowing where the caves came out — honestly, Cory — at least I didn't —"

"Me either," said Kev and Maxie together.

"Initiation into *what?*" demanded Bip.

"Well, into the club," said Peter. "Why not? Then she could be Chess Master and —"

"Yes," said Maxie, "that's it. And it would make up for everything."

"Then let's vote on it," went on Peter, "shall we? Everybody in favor of letting Cory into the club, say 'Aye.'"

And everybody did say "Aye," except Bip and Augie, which didn't matter, pointed out Peter, because it was four against two. "But I don't see what's your reason. She'll only be here a few more weeks, and why couldn't she be in for just that little bit?"

"Oh, well, then," said Augie, and shrugged.

"So then you're in," said Peter.

However, surprisingly, even to Cory herself, "No, thanks," she said, getting up. "And I'm not mad any more. But I don't want to be taken in just because I'm only going to be here a little while longer."

In the uncertain light she caught Peter's eye, and he gave her a funny quick look that seemed to her to mean that if he and she could have changed places, he would have refused too.

The last shreds of mist were winding off into the distance, losing themselves under the darkening blue of the sky. One star came out, and then another. The wind was rising a little in the pines. Cory, panting, scrabbled up the side of the gorge to the path that led round toward Tarnhelm — Peter's shortcut. And it was when she came to Peter's little dug-out place where they had taken shelter from the storm that she first heard a voice calling.

"Co-o-ory! Co-o-o-ory!" There was an edge of stark, broken fear in that cry.

It was Fergie, and it seemed as if she was over by the cliff wall. Cory started running, made her way quickly up the wooded slope below the wall, and climbed over just in time to see Fergie hurrying away. She called out, Fergie turned, and in another moment Cory was en-

184

veloped in a pair of tightening arms. Fergie was almost weeping.

"Oh, darling, darling — yer grandmother and Andrew and I looked down and saw that the tide was in — right in at the cave where Andrew said he'd hear-rd you and the rest of the children about a half an hour ago. He didn't know whether you'd stayed down there or not. And we tried to call the Hawthornes, and there's nobody home — or at least nobody answered, and we couldn't see you down in the gorge, nor over at the Hawthornes' anywhere, nor down on the beach, and we were just fr-rantic. We none of us knew the names of the other children, so we couldn't phone their parents — oh, ye should just have hear-rd yer granny! She said she would never forgive herself if anything — oh, and Andrew's gone. He went over to the Hawthornes' to see if he could see ye. Look, there he is now, back again, or maybe it's yer Uncle Dur-rk. No, it's both of them —"

Two sets of headlights swung up along the drive, far across the lawn, and now Fergie and Cory started back toward the house.

"But Fergie, we were all *right*. We were in the caves with the tide in, but the caves are all dry and safe back under the cliffs, no matter *how* far the waves come up. Because, Fergie, guess what! You keep going in under, and *keep* going in under, and it's like rooms, and we went through such darkness as you never saw, and came out on the side of the chasm — on the Tarnhelm side of it — the big one you looked down in to find us, but I guess we hadn't come out yet. So when we did, we talked for a while and then the others went off home and I climbed back up and came right along Peter's shortcut as easy and safe as you please —"

But Fergie kept shaking her head and tchk-ing.

"It's yer granny," she'd say off and on all the way up to the house in the deepening dusk that was now almost night. "She's that upset — ye never saw the like of it! Not that Andrew and I weren't, but she went all to pieces. It was terrible — just terrible —"

They went in at the back door and, as Fergie turned to lock it and Cory paused for a moment before going into the kitchen, bracing herself to face Mrs. Van Heusen, they heard Andrew's and Uncle Dirk's voices mingled, and then:

"But I cannot *endure* things like this, I tell you," exclaimed Mrs. Van Heusen. "I simply cannot be asked to face one crisis like this after another. No one has any right to ask me! You don't *know* what I've been through since five-thirty, and now it's after six. I am the child's guardian while she's here, Dirk Van Heusen — not you — and I have a responsibility to Stephanie. No, I will *not* face such a thing as this again —"

Why, it sounds exactly like Stephanie, Cory thought,

Grandmother just like Stephanie in a play. "I cannot *endure* — I simply cannot be *asked* — I will *not* face — " etc., etc.

And then Uncle Dirk's voice:

"But why keep on making such a ridiculous fuss, Mother, when I've *told* you the caves are perfectly safe —"

"And Peter's home, Mrs. Van Heusen," put in Andrew, "and the other children were just leaving the Hawthornes'. They said Cory's on her way up."

"Stephanie and I and all the young ones around here," went on Uncle Dirk, irritated and impatient, "used to play down in those caves all the time, and you know it. There's no possible danger — it's exactly the sort of thing kids love. Surely you remember that hole on the side of the gorge where we used to go in and out —"

But she did not remember it, said Mrs. Van Heusen (they must all have been out in the hall, for now Cory and Fergie were in the kitchen and the voices were coming from beyond the breakfast room). She did *not* remember. She happened to have suffered agony for this past half hour and she could not face this sort of thing ever again — she would not forget that moment for the rest of her life when she had looked over the cliff and seen the waves crashing in at the mouth of the cave. "No, Dirk, I've made up my mind. I've been undecided, but not any longer. I shall not broach the subject to Stephanie about having the child here indefinitely — and that's my final decision."

"Well, at least, Fergie," said Cory when she got into bed that night, "at least now that's settled — no more suspense about it. But Uncle Dirk doesn't want me to go. He told me tonight that if it were up to him, he'd keep me. And he said he'll miss having me here like anything, and he'll miss our chess games in the evening. You don't suppose he said that just to be polite, do you?"

"No," said Fergie. "No, darling, I do not. He doesn't say things just to be polite. He said it because he meant it."

Thirteen

NOT LONG after this, Uncle Dirk took Cory to San Francisco and they spent a whole day at the park, seeing the museum and the Japanese tea garden and the aquarium and the museum of natural history, just as he had promised. They stayed that night with friends of his, in a house high on a hill where you could look out over the million lights of the city and the long, stretched-out necklace of lights moving across the bridge from Berkeley and Oakland glimmering on the far side of the dark water.

The next day they went out to the beach to have breakfast at the Cliff House and watch the seals on the seal rocks. Then they rode a cable car up one steep hill and down another, so that Cory could get the real flavor of San Francisco: the high, narrow-faced houses set right against each other, mounting or descending in stair steps, some terribly shabby and ugly, others elegant in the extreme — town houses with fabulous furnishings, Uncle Dirk said, and each of these with its small, beautifully kept garden, and always the little Greek or Italian or Japanese or Chinese grocery down at the corner where one could buy almost any tantalizing food that came to mind. And then the vistas! Every street one passed seemed to swoop directly into the bay, blue beyond description, set with islands and slung with long graceful spans of bridges. It took Cory's breath away.

"I love it — this city!" said Uncle Dirk. "There's not another like it anywhere, not even remotely like it —"

"Then why don't you live here, Uncle Dirk?"

"Because it already has too many architects."

They explored Chinatown with its crowded, narrow streets and its shops filled with silks and lacquers and carvings and strange foods, herbs and pressed duck and dried sea horses, and from which such fantastic smells floated as Cory could never have imagined —

"Kind of like decayed mushrooms," decided Uncle Dirk.

After a late lunch at Fishermen's Wharf, they went for a boat ride on the wind-whipped bay, swept under the bridge "— a *mile* up, it must be!" shouted Cory, and along by the iron-colored rocks of the islands, where the waves dashed themselves in constant up-heaval.

"Is this all right?" Uncle Dirk leaned over to say into her ear. They were sitting at the rail and he had been pointing out to her where he had gone, as a young man, on the ferryboats back and forth from Berkeley when he had been there at college. "Are you having a good time?"

"Uncle Dirk, it's been — it's been just —" and then a plunge of the boat and a pelting gust of wind tore the words out of her mouth, but she looked at him and slid her cold hand into his warm one, and that seemed to be all the answer he needed.

The following Saturday, Cory and the Explorers got into the station wagon with their lunches, and Andrew took them along the coast to Big Sur, singing Andrew's songs as well as their own all the way, and they ate beside the river and then hiked up to the falls high in the redwoods. Other days Cory went with Peter and the rest of them over to Point Lobos to the bird rocks and the sea lion rocks and out around the cypress trails. She saw the Explorers often after school, and they were together now until almost dark down on the beach below Peter's house and in the caves. It was as if she had never lived anywhere else, never had any life but this nor any friends but these. She refused to think of the day when Stephanie would come to take her away.

She went with Peter up to Laurel's house again to get Mrs. Hawthorne's skirt when it was ready, and after that she often went alone to sit there and talk while Laurel did her weaving. She told Laurel about Fergie and Andrew and Grandmother and Uncle Dirk, and about Stephanie and living in New York. And Laurel told her about when she was Cory's age, going to school in Carmel and then later to the university in Berkeley.

"Why, that's where Uncle Dirk went. Maybe you were there when he was."

They were perfectly comfortable together, and Cory would help get lunch and then stay for the afternoon. They did not always talk, and when Laurel was busy answering letters, Cory would read. Laurel had kept all the books she'd ever treasured, and had a whole collection of children's books illustrated by an artist named Arthur Rackham — *Peter Pan* and Andersen's *Fairy Tales* and *The Wind in the Willows, Poor Cecco*, and *Gulliver's Travels*, and lots of others, and it was then that Cory grew to know the intoxicating smell of English books. Whenever she caught it after that, she would think of that room high on the mountainside, long and airy and full of pale green light, and Laurel sitting at her desk writing. She would hear the quick whisper of her pen on the paper, boughs moving outside the windows, a woodpecker tapping, squirrels scolding, sparks snapping on the hearth on cold days, and would see again the colors of Rackham's illustrations, rich and subtle, deep and pale, and the enchanted maidens of the fairy tales who, to Cory, all looked like Laurel.

"What is your Uncle Dirk like, Cory?"

"Well, he's not the Black Prince at all, except in looks. He usually beats me at chess, but a few times I've beaten him, and it seems to tickle him when I do. He seems more pleased when I win than when he does, but we both put up a good fight."

"The Black Prince," said Laurel.

"Yes. He's very dark, with a straight nose and a lot of almost black hair and very blue eyes. Fergie says that's a Celtic combination, and I like it. Celtic means Scotch or Irish or Welsh. Grandmother says Stephanie takes after the Austrian side of the family —"

"She's blond," said Laurel. "Very striking."

"Oh, do you know her?"

"You've described her to me."

"Yes, I'd forgotten. Uncle Dirk has nice hands. I like the way he holds the chess pieces and puts them down. Do you ever notice people's hands? Some hands make me feel peculiar and that I wouldn't like that person, but I suppose that isn't fair. I think you have beautiful hands — I wish my fingernails were smooth and oval-shaped like yours."

"But if you're always exploring, going through caves and hunting for shells and rocks and climbing up cliffs, you couldn't possibly keep your nails like mine. Nobody could expect you to."

"Grandmother does. She says I never think about how I look, and I don't, I guess. She's very particular. I think I'm a bother to her, but there're only three more days — only I don't think about that."

"Three more days," said Laurel.

"Yes, and it's a funny thing about Grandmother. She said this morning at breakfast that she hoped I hadn't been too unhappy here, and she put her arm around me and drew me over to her. I almost thought by the way she looked at me that she wanted to say that she gave in, and that she would ask Stephanie if I could stay. But she didn't. And I could almost see the words sort of pressed up behind her face, but she wouldn't let them out. She *wouldn't*, even though they wanted to come. And Fergie just stood there with some plates, watching Grandmother, and I could see she was wishing and wishing as hard as I was. But it wasn't any use. I *think* she cares about me, but —"

"It would complicate things," said Laurel. "It would be a worry to her."

"Do you know her?" asked Cory in surprise.

"We've met."

Now Laurel got up and went to the piano and began playing and singing something.

> *"Alas, my love, you do me wrong*
> *To cast me off discourteously,*
> *And I have lo-oved you so long,*
> *Delighting in your company.*

> *"Greensleeves was all my joy,*
> *Greensleeves was my-y delight.*
> *Greensleeves was my heart of gold,*
> *And who but Lady Greensleeves!"*

"But that's *it*, Laurel — that's *it* — the song you sang the first day Peter brought me here, and I told Fergie and Andrew I knew I'd heard it before!"

Laurel turned on the piano bench.

"It's an old Elizabethan song. Where have you heard it?"

"I don't know. I've thought and thought, and I can't remember. Not at school — not at home. I mean, not back East. Stephanie's never sung it, I'm *sure*. It seems to me I heard it after I came to Tarnhelm."

"Did somebody sing it there?"

"No, but I've heard it — I know I have. Just the music." Cory sat there, concentrating, and then she looked up, her face lighting. "Laurel — I *know*. It was my dream — you remember I told you when I was sick that I had that big, long dream? About the enormous dark room with the bars of moonlight coming in? That was when I heard it, terribly sad and far away, but so beautiful I never wanted it to stop —"

"But Cory, how could you hear music in a dream that you would recognize afterwards, when you say you've never heard it before in your life? I mean, how would it be in your head for you to dream of it?"

"I don't know — but it just was."

Laurel continued to sit at the piano as if she were thinking, her hands in her lap, and then, almost absently, as if her mind were on something else, began playing again. But presently she stopped.

"Cory, I'm going away."

Cory stared at her in shocked silence.

"You mean for *good*, Laurel?"

"No, for a few months, I think. I'm not certain just how long."

"And you haven't said anything all day."

"I had the letter just after you were here last week. A friend of mine wants me to come and stay with her in Taos, in New Mexico, and then we're going to travel around for a while. I haven't been away anywhere for a long time."

"When are you going?" Strange, thought Cory, that

her heart should feel so heavy when she herself would be leaving soon.

"Very early, the morning after tomorrow. Some neighbors are coming by about six-thirty to pick me up and take me to the airport in Monterey, and I'll fly in to San Francisco and take the jet from there—"

"I'll miss you! I'm glad you've stayed this long. It seems as if everything's coming to an end at once."

Laurel got up and went over to the bookshelves.

"I have something I want to give you. It's a book I bought in France several years ago." She drew out a large, thin, paper-covered book that had been lying on top of the others. It was titled *The Lady and the Unicorn*, and there was a colored picture on the cover of a unicorn and a lion with banners, and a lady between them. As Laurel turned over the pages, Cory saw that on each page was a richly colored picture of the lion and the lady and the unicorn doing different things. "It's a book of tapestries. I saw them in the Cluny Museum in Paris and I thought they were so beautiful that I bought this book so that I could look at them whenever I wanted." She reached out and lifted up the little silver amulet that hung on the chain around Cory's neck. "Because the unicorn means something special to you, I want you to have it."

"Thank you, Laurel." Cory opened the cover and saw written on the flyleaf, *For Cory — in memory of our happy times together — yours always, with love, Laurel,* and she looked up. "But — won't we ever see each other again? Is that what you mean?"

"Of course we'll see each other. We *must* — next summer when you come back. I'll be looking forward to that, and I'll have so much to tell you —"

"Well, but I don't know if I'll be coming back. I hope so. I don't know which I've liked best, being with Fergie and Andrew and Uncle Dirk, or being up here with you. But one thing I do know, I don't want to go to Connecticut and start trying to live in the country again and getting to like it and then having to give it all up the way we did last time. Everything always seems to be starting but never finishing. Why is that? Will you write to me, Laurel? Here — I'll put my address down and you can send me postcards whenever you have a chance. And I'll write to you. I promise you I will — I mean when you get back."

On the way home that afternoon, with her book done up in brown paper under her arm, Cory turned it all over in her mind. Just think, she wasn't going to see Laurel, perhaps ever again. Laurel had been different today, quieter. Wasn't she happy any more? But perhaps she *was* lonely up there in her house in the forest, even though she would never admit it. How odd it was to feel that she knew Laurel almost as well as she knew Stephanie, and yet not quite. Not quite.

For instance, just before she left she had said:

"It's Grandmother I'm not quite sure of, about coming back, I mean. But Laurel — if you wanted me to, perhaps I could come and visit you next summer. You could write Stephanie —"

But curiously enough, a sudden startled look came into Laurel's eyes.

"You would be in Connecticut by then —"

"That wouldn't matter. But it's all right, if you don't think it would be convenient for you. I only thought — we've had so much fun, that maybe you would —"

"I *would*, Cory! I *would* want you!" Laurel put her hands on Cory's shoulders and then all at once drew her close. "I've wished so many times you could just stay. It isn't that. It's only that Stephanie would think it strange —"

"*Why* would she?"

And then the subject had gotten changed somehow, though Cory for the life of her couldn't remember how, unless it was because of talking about Stephanie. But she had a feeling, when she tried to get it all back, that nothing had been settled, and the worst part was not being able to understand Laurel. Grownups were so puzzling, all of them, every one, except Fergie and

Andrew. They had gotten after her once or twice about something, but she'd always understood. They had never puzzled her — they had never hurt her, not once.

After what seemed to be only a few minutes, Cory looked up in astonishment to find herself almost at the Smallwoods'. She had gone clear down through the forest, hardly conscious of where she had been walking, then out of the forest and across the fields. Now all at once there was Toby, the Smallwoods' big white bulldog, barking at her. She called to him and he stopped at once and came to her, grinning in foolish delight, his stub of a tail wagging his whole chunky body. His great round brown marble eyes shone up at her moistly, his tongue lolled, and he pushed fondly against her with his whole weight while she talked to him. Then suddenly Mr. Smallwood came out of the house.

"Well, hel-*lo*, Cory — you on your way home? Come on, hop in the car, I'll take you. Hattie's been awfully sick, but I just now got one of the neighbors to come and sit with her while I go into town for groceries. Wouldn't want to leave her alone —"

"I'm sorry, Mr. Smallwood — is she —?" Cory was about to get into the front of the Dowager when Toby almost knocked her over; he flopped over the top of the seat into the back and there he settled, panting in triumph and smiling broadly as if he were overjoyed at the prospect of a drive.

"Well, she seems a lot better —" Mr. Smallwood started up the motor, backed carefully, swung around, and away they went down the long bumpy road to the highway. "She seems a lot better, practically her old self, but I don't want to go taking any chances leaving her alone. If she started getting feverish again the way she was night before last, she might slip out of bed and start wandering around and goodness only knows where she might get to —"

"Oh, I know, Mr. Smallwood, I know ex-*zactly* —"

"But she's going to be just fine. Seems to me," said Mr. Smallwood, "that's a fairly long distance for a young one like you to come all by yourself — clear up into the forest and back. I don't know as I —"

"Oh, but I don't mind. I love it. When you're anxious to see somebody, and then going through meadows and forest — why, it's — I don't know, it never seems long at all. And lots of times Peter comes. Of course, we never go the long way around. It seems as if Peter knows a shortcut to everything. The first time he took me up to the mountain, he showed me how you could go up behind Tarnhelm to where that house was going to be built and then right down to the highway from there instead of back in the other direction to the Tarnhelm gate —"

"You mean your Uncle Dirk's house? Funny thing he never finished that place, but I suppose as long as he wasn't going to get married after all, there wasn't any use going ahead. Kind of a sorry thing, that was. And he's never married anybody. Hattie'n I always wondered —"

When Toby lunged forward on one of the rolling bounces the Dowager took on an especially deep rut, and tucked his nose behind her ear and gave her cheek a loving swipe with his tongue, Cory silently hunched up her shoulder and wiped the wet place on her sleeve.

"But I don't know," continued Mr. Smallwood, "your Uncle Dirk might not've been too easy to get on with in those days. Kind of an indifferent young fellow, he used to be. Though nowadays, you wouldn't want to meet a nicer person — always courteous to me, and asks after both of us. I hope you didn't pay too much attention to what Hattie said that day we brought you out — she lives in the past a lot —"

Cory did not know what else Mr. Smallwood talked about, though he went on fairly steadily, nor did she say anything until she saw the beginning of the Tarn-helm wall.

"Here it is, Mr. Smallwood." She put her hand on his arm. "This is where you let me off, right below where the house was going to be. This is where the shortcut is. Thank you ever so much."

She stood watching the car going round the curve, and saw Toby's big head lean out of the side of the Dowager to catch a last glimpse of her, his uncut ears flapping in the gentle breeze of its passage.

"Fergie and Andrew, did you ever know Uncle Dirk was going to be married? Did you know that was his house — the beginnings of it — up there behind Tarn-helm?"

Fergie turned from the stove, her eyes widening.

"Why, no, darling. Whoever told ye such a thing as that?"

"Mr. Smallwood."

"Ah," said Andrew.

He and Fergie were silent, then Fergie turned again.

"I wouldn't bring it up to him, Cory dear. If he'd ever wanted to say anything about it to any of us, he'd have done it long before this."

Fourteen

THE LATE afternoon sun cast mellow, coppery-golden rays across the sea into the gorge, where Peter and Cory had been what they called "making up history." At last, having exhausted their imaginations for the time being, they got up onto a rock and sat there with their arms locked around their knees and gazed peacefully out over the sea. Cory watched and listened. She wanted to soak up every detail so that she could hold it all very clearly in her memory until the time when she might possibly come back again.

Directly opposite her in the top of one of the smaller pines, she saw a large gray squirrel busily intent on some household chore, and a red-breasted nuthatch making its way along the underside of a branch, gathering insects as he went. The trees in the gorge were all pink on their western sides. Down on the shore a burnished covey of sandpipers were twinkling along on their stick-like legs pecking up fleas like mad from the wet sand in the wake of each receding wave. The waves flashed gold on their crests as they curved.

Now it's all over, thought Cory. The whole experience of living at Tarnhelm had gone in a trice as if it had never been — no, as if it had taken no more than a moment to happen. How mysterious that was. And there was no way of holding it back, of keeping something perfect, any more than you could hold water in the cupped palms of your hands.

"Tell you what," said Peter all at once, "I'll show you our treasures if you like, Cory. You're going in a couple of days, so it doesn't matter, your not being a member of the club. Though of course you *were* voted in —"

"Would you show me, Peter? Especially the carved box that I think is Uncle Dirk's? Have you opened it yet?"

"No. The others wanted to bang it open, but I wouldn't let them because I've been thinking about it. If it *is* your uncle's, then we shouldn't open it. I thought I'd ask him about it if I ever had a good chance, but I haven't."

A rich glow filled the cave, lighting the side halfway to the back, where Peter went to a large rock, knelt, and dragged a sack from behind it. Out of it he pulled what looked like part of a woman's head and neck and shoulders carved in wood, but split on a slant, with the features so worn and rounded that they were scarcely recognizable.

"Why, it looks like a ship's figurehead, Peter. Just the top —"

"I know. We found it wedged in the rocks way up beyond Tarnhelm where nobody ever climbs. Just think where it's been — where it could have come from. A shipwreck, I bet, maybe fifty or a hundred years ago. And then here're a lot of shells we've found that we keep in this box, and these are whales' earbones, I think. And this green glass ball is a Japanese fisherman's — they tie them to their nets to keep them afloat. Just think, it's come clear across the Pacific! And *this* —" He drew out a large animal skull, and Cory stared. "I betcha *this* must be a mountain lion's —"

"But Andrew says they don't come this close to civilization," protested Cory anxiously. "They stay *way back up in the hills* —"

"Well, I don't know. Anyhow, we found this skull right down there in the gorge — not in the rocks as if it could have washed there from somewhere else, but right down *there*. So maybe they come down at night. Of course, it could be a horse's skull, or a cow's, but I'd lots rather think it's a mountain lion's. And this shoe box we keep our dues in, and the constitution and our

206

rules of order." He shook it. "Five and a half dollars we've got. We keep wanting to spend them on something but we can't agree what we really want the most. Then Bip found this pearl necklace on the beach, but I don't know if they're real pearls or not, and I found this ring. See, it's an emeral' — I bet it's valuable. I'm going to take it to a jeweler's one day and find out. And now — here's the carved box." He pulled it from the sack and Cory took it.

It was dark brown, about three inches high, ten inches long and five and a half inches across, and it was covered, top and sides, with small flowers carved out of the dark wood, very finely and beautifully carved, with each petal, each leaf clear and precise. There was no lock, but because the alternate dampness and heat of the caves had swelled the wood and warped it, it was as tightly closed as if it had been locked fast.

"Who found it, Peter?"

"I did, about two weeks ago. I was hunting for a good place to keep our treasure, because I wasn't satisfied with the other place, and I found it right down in behind that rock — there, where I got the sack from just now. It was jammed in underneath. And it's got something in it. Shake it."

Cory heard a soft, sliding sound.

"Oh, Peter — what d'you suppose? Would you let

me take it up to Uncle Dirk? And if it isn't his, I promise you I'll bring it back. Oh, but I'm sure it must be — I'm sure this is his carving. You can tell it's hand-carved because the pattern isn't regular and each flower is just a little different from the others. He told me all about carving when we went to the museum in San Francisco. *Could* I take it to him, Peter?"

"No!" said an angry voice. "Don't you let her. I *told* you, Peter Hawthorne — we'll never get it back!" It was Bip.

Cory looked up and around, and there, standing at the entrance of the cave, was Bip, with Augie coming up behind her, and then Kev and Maxie peered in. They looked astonished, staring at Peter and Cory and then at the open sack with their treasures spread out and the box in Cory's lap.

"You've got a nerve, showing her all our stuff," said Augie slowly and sternly and with a certain dignity. "It's our stuff too — you didn't have any right." Everybody came in and sat down except Bip, who continued to stand at the cave's entrance.

Peter was silent for a moment and Cory could see that he knew Augie was right.

"O.K.," he said. "I'm sorry, Augie. I guess I shouldn't have, without a vote, even if I am president and supposed to make decisions. But she's going day after tomorrow, and she *was* voted in, and I didn't know if you kids were coming up or not, and I thought she ought to show the box to her uncle before she goes. That way, it'd save *us* taking it up to him."

"I'm sure it must be Uncle Dirk's, Bip. I'll bet you anything he was the one who put it there —"

"Why would he?" demanded Bip scornfully. "I never heard anything so silly. Why would a grown-up man hide a box in a cave? Besides, it's ours — we found it. Finders keepers."

"No, I found it," reminded Peter. "Though of course, anything that one Explorer finds belongs to everybody. That's part of the rules."

"But you know, I've been thinking," said Cory. "Isn't this Tarnhelm property you're on? Grandmother's land comes right out to the cliffs over there by the sea and over here to the gorge, so all these caves are *in* her land, so wouldn't anything found here really belong to her, or to Uncle Dirk? If you say this box is yours, wouldn't you be stealing?"

Silence, while Bip studied Cory.

"I told you we shouldn't have let her in!" she burst out.

"But I think she's right," said Kev.

"Yes," said Maxie, "and besides, if it isn't your uncle's, Cory, at least maybe he can open it for us without wrecking the box. I can't wait to know what's inside."

They would vote, said Peter; and so they did, and once more only Bip held out. She turned away with hostile eyes and went back down into the gorge.

"Why won't she be friends?" asked Cory. "I wish she would. I'll hate going away with —" But, self-conscious, she could not finish. She felt it was like a curse which meant she might never come back.

"Oh, heck, why always expect everybody to like you?" demanded Peter impatiently. "Hardly *anybody* has everybody liking him, and what difference does it make? Bip'll get over it. She never takes to anything right off the bat — or any person either."

Fifteen

IT WAS almost dark, with the moon already climbing the blue-green sky, when Cory ran across the lawn at the side of Tarnhelm. A wind had sprung up so that the shaggy black giants around the porch were plowing their arms up and down and murmuring and sighing together. There was a light coming from the kitchen windows, but not the bright one that meant Fergie was there getting dinner. This was the soft light of the table lamp which maybe Grandmother or Uncle Dirk had turned on, because Fergie and Andrew had left about three o'clock that afternoon. They had gone to see Fergie's aunt in San Francisco about signing some family business papers, and would have to be gone overnight, Fergie had said.

Cory was eager to show Uncle Dirk the carved box and perhaps, if it were his, ask him to tell her why he had hidden it in the cave. She fished for the key under the piled wood in a secret hollow she and Andrew and Fergie had agreed on, and when she came into the warm kitchen, she saw a note on the table where her place was set all by itself.

Dear Cory — Fergie left stew to heat up in the double boiler, and I've put a potato to bake in the oven for you. There's a salad in the refrigerator and also your dessert. Your grandmother is upstairs in her room with a bad headache and doesn't want to be disturbed so that she can try to get some sleep. I'll be in later — meantime take care of yourself, spalpeen, eat a good dinner and get to bed on time.

Love —
Uncle Dirk

Cory sighed and sat down at the table with the box in front of her. She was terribly disappointed not to be able to show it to him. How still the house is, she thought, just a touch frightened at being in the big stone place practically alone, what with Mrs. Van Heusen asleep. The house was a hollow of stillness inside the restless, leaping, rushing wind. She got up, lit the flame under the double boiler, put on Fergie's padded mit, and opened the oven door to feel the baked potato — it was almost done. She got her salad from the refrigerator and saw that Fergie had made apricot cobbler (I'll put a big scoop of ice cream on *that*, Cory told herself, beginning to cheer up). Then she took the box and went upstairs to get a book to read while she ate.

Uncle Dirk had left the lights on in the hall and one or two lamps in the living room, where the radio was playing just loudly enough to be heard as she went by. That was so I wouldn't feel lonely, Cory thought. Oh, Uncle Dirk — I'll *miss* him, and Fergie and Andrew and Laurel.

She turned and went upstairs, pausing for a moment outside Mrs. Van Heusen's door. She heard a sigh, the whisper of a silken comforter, and there was the tinkle of a spoon on a glass.

"Grandmother?" said Cory. "I just want to tell you I'm home."

Silence. Then a muffled voice:

"All right, dear. Now go and eat, please, and don't call me for anything. I have a dreadful headache — I just want to get to sleep."

"Yes. I'm awfully sorry."

Cory tiptoed along to her own room and put the box on the table beside her bed. I know what I'll do, she said to herself, I'll come up after I've done the dishes and I'll build a fire in my fireplace and get into bed and read the unicorn book. And maybe Laurel will phone and say goodbye.

Andrew had taught Cory well the art of crisscrossing kindling over crushed-up newspaper, then laying the heavier pieces on top in such a way that they did not smash the structure of kindling nor shut out the air. Flames sprang up at once, licking their way fiercely in and out, and there was a great snapping as the larger pieces caught. She was pleased. It was a most successful fire; not Peter nor Uncle Dirk nor even Andrew himself — and he was a champion fire builder — could have done better. Presently she put on two small logs, then got into her pajamas and climbed into bed. And it was so snug there in her lamplit room with the fire crackling and the wind swirling outside that she wanted only to sit contentedly and rather drowsily watching the fire and listening.

Then she happened to glance up and saw how the shadows and leaping gleams gave Stephanie's mask the strangest expression — half-smiling, but not a happy smile. It seemed rather to be mysterious, teasing, even mocking, and the eyes appeared to be half-closed. Cory did not like that expression at all, and she looked down suddenly and opened *The Lady and the Unicorn* and began studying the pictures.

Each was of a tapestry, and each tapestry was meant to illustrate one of the five senses. For Sight, the Lady, sitting on a blue island surrounded by innumerable little flowers and animals, held in her right hand a mirror in which the unicorn, nearby, saw itself reflected. Its front hoofs were on the Lady's lap and her left palm rested on its neck. A lion stood on her other side, and there were banners and shields on either hand. For Hearing, the Lady played a small organ; for Smell, she held in her two hands a crown of flowers; for Feeling, she caressed the unicorn; for Taste, she took a sweetmeat from a cup presented by a waiting maid. And in each tapestry the lion stood on one side, and the unicorn on the other. Then there was a last tapestry which did not seem to fit in with the others at all: the Lady stood in front of a tent, and across the top of the tent above the entrance was inscribed in capitals the French words, "A MON SEUL DESIR." "To my one desire," Laurel had said those words meant, or perhaps, "Toward my one desire."

Toward my one desire. Cory looked up again and watched how the constantly changing lights and shadows made that curious smile on Stephanie's carved lips seem to deepen, then to fade and vanish so that she was expressionless as usual. Then there it was again — that smile — more mocking than ever. My one desire — to stay here, Stephanie, and never, never go away. To eat with Fergie and Andrew in the kitchen and be with them and Grandmother and Uncle Dirk until I grow up and have a home of my own someday, and to have Grandmother just the way she was that night when Uncle Dirk and I first played chess. And to be Peter's friend and to go up and see Laurel whenever I like and to be *her* real friend for always and always. That's my desire.

Cory let *The Lady and the Unicorn* fall onto the counterpane and curled her fingers around her own little silver unicorn. "I wish," she whispered. "I *wish* — I *wish* —" Then she put her head back against the pillows and closed her eyes. Sight, Hearing, Smell, Feeling, thought Cory. *Taste* of chocolate — that was the medicine the doctor had given her when she was sick; *smell* of dust and dry wood, of a stuffy, closed-in place, a smell with a kind of camphory, aromatic edge to it; *touch* of smooth, hand-rubbed wood carved into chess pieces — beautiful chess pieces that were like no others — magical chess pieces with unicorns for knights. *Sight* of velvety darkness and then moonlight slanting across a bare floor. *Sound* of (and this was what had been in Cory's mind the whole time; this was what had made her think of all the other things) — sound of "Greensleeves," slow and grave and sad, played as Laurel had played it, on a piano.

Cory sat up, rigid, erect, both hands clasped tightly around the silver unicorn, staring at the mask of Stephanie, whose dark, hollow, sightless eyes stared back out of a face that now seemed almost alive. She understood at last. *She had actually been hearing someone play.* Uncle Dirk had been playing on the piano downstairs, but softly, because it was nighttime and she was sick in bed upstairs. That had *not* been a dream. Stephanie and Laurel on the beach, yes. But not the big, dark room. That was real, and the chess set with its unicorns for knights was real, and no wonder Uncle Dirk had said she was bewitched to have had such a dream as this about a place and about things he knew existed but which Cory, if she was telling the truth, had never seen in her life.

What was it Mr. Smallwood had said about Mrs. Smallwood? "If she starts getting feverish again — if her temperature starts going up — she might get out of bed and wander around and no knowing where to —"

Cory slid from under the covers, put on her slippers and her robe, and padded over to the door. Her heart was beating furiously; she knew what she must do if she possibly could, yet she was not at all certain why she must. She shut the door behind her.

In the hall, where she had left the light on, she went without hesitation to Uncle Dirk's workroom. She crossed directly to the door that opened into the little hall where, on her left, the tower stairs went up and, ahead of her, stood that other door. She went forward across moonlight falling through a single window, and turned the knob. Yes, here was the dusty, closed-in smell and the camphory, aromatic odor. This was the

218

smell she remembered, and here were stairs descending into the dark.

She felt for the light switch and turned it on, and when she got to the bottom of the stairs saw that her dream had indeed not been a dream.

There were the tall, narrow windows set deep in the outer stones through which rays of moonlight that other night had slanted through so silvery-bright as to seem almost substantial — as if they might have been cool and firm to the touch. The big room was freezing cold, so that Cory shivered as she crossed to the cabinets under the windows and to the chess set laid out on top of one of them. But she did not know if she shivered from cold, from fear of Uncle Dirk's return, or from some growing expectancy which she could not have put into words but was clearly aware of.

There was the chess set with the pieces standing at random on the board as if in the midst of acting out a story, just as she remembered leaving them. There were the rooks carved in the shape of castle towers, the bishops with their little miters on their heads, the kings and queens dressed in royal robes and looking out from tiny faces under their delicately carved crowns. And, most perfect of all, there were the four unicorns (two light and two dark) rearing on their hind legs with their front feet pawing the air and slender horns spiraling upward from their foreheads.

They were all so enchanting that Cory picked them up one at a time, studying them minutely and smoothing them with delighted fingers. And as she did so, she saw that the expressions on the faces of the light king and queen were happy and that those on the faces of the dark royal pair were stern and unsmiling. Their heads were set at quite different angles: the dark pair were looking straight ahead, cold and grave, with their hands clasped in front of them, while the light pair were looking around at one another and the left hand of the queen was about to take the right hand of the king.

Surely it meant something. What could it possibly mean? What had Uncle Dirk been thinking as he carved them? Was there a story in this?

Cory moved the light king and queen together so that their little hands touched, and now there was such a distinct feeling of gay, warm tenderness between them that it was almost miraculous. Then all at once she put the light queen near the dark king — and how sad it was! The queen was trying to mend some quarrel with him, trying to coax him back to her, but he would not listen, would not look at her, and stared straight ahead so that one knew it was hopeless. He would never change. Quickly Cory moved the queen over to her own love again — and all was well. *Let* the two dark, miserable ones stay together, she thought. They were fit for one another, stubborn, unfeeling, deaf and blind to reason and tenderness, intent only upon their own pride and dignity.

Cory picked up the light queen and, with the small wooden figure pressed to her chest, turned and stared around the vast room. This was the part of Tarnhelm, she realized, that jutted out toward the sea.

Now, on a sudden impulse, she turned back and opened the cabinet door. She reached out a hand and the first object she drew forth she recognized at once with such a shock that a bolt of burning leaped through her.

What she held was the mask of Laurel Woodford.

There was the broad, clear forehead with the serene, almost level brows, the slender nose, the wide mouth faintly smiling in precisely Laurel's way. There could not possibly be any mistake. And when Cory bent to look inside the cabinet, she found three more masks of Laurel — Laurel in different moods, as if Uncle Dirk were a painter painting his favorite subject again and again, a face he never tired of, whose different aspects he would never finish exploring.

It was Laurel Uncle Dirk had been engaged to, and it was for her he had been going to build that house up behind Tarnhelm — surely that was it? And this was why Uncle Dirk and Grandmother never said anything when Cory, two or three times, had tried to tell them of the new friend she had made and about Laurel's house in the forest. They changed the subject; they didn't seem to care about hearing — yet, Cory remembered now, she hadn't thought anything of it at the time. They seemed indifferent, and yet to *think* of all that must have been going through their heads! And Laurel — what must have been going on in Laurel's mind when she questioned Cory very casually, yet nevertheless closely, about Grandmother's feelings. *And Uncle Dirk —*

"The Black Prince," Laurel had repeated thoughtfully when Cory had described him to her. "The Black Prince."

She took up the mask of Laurel she had first found, and clasped it to her. She wanted it! She wanted this and the little light queen to take back to New York. Yet she could never ask Uncle Dirk for them in a million years and of course she couldn't steal them. With the mask and the small figure still in her hands, she wandered about the great, high-ceilinged place which was not simply a storeroom but a vast workshop, where it seemed that Uncle Dirk must have been making all the furniture his and Laurel's home would need when they married. Here were chairs, a dining table, several cabinets, two bedsteads, one large chest and a smaller one, a dressing table, some bookcases, and a game table with a chess board inlaid.

Cory was so cold that her hands and feet were numb,

so now she put the mask of Laurel back where she had found it, and then bent over the chess set for the last time.

"Goodbye, unicorns," she said. "Goodbye, Laurel."

A moment later she was going up the stairs; she switched off the lights, and just as she crossed the workroom, she heard footsteps along the main hallway and Uncle Dirk singing a melancholy little song to himself, under his breath, about a man who lived in San Domingo and whose name was Oh, By Jingo. It was his favorite song when he was concentrating and didn't even know he was singing. Now his voice faded, for he had apparently gone into his bedroom. Cory very quietly shut the workroom door behind her, crossed the hall, shut her own bedroom door, and got into bed and turned out the light.

She lay there shivering, her heart beating like fury. *Why did you do that?* she asked herself. Why didn't you go in to him and tell him what you'd done? *But I can't — I can't!* I went where I wasn't supposed to (now Uncle Dirk passed her door again and she heard the hall light click off). If he hadn't cared about my knowing about Laurel, that they were going to be married and that that mask up in the tower was going to be her, and that those were her poems, he'd have told me long ago. And if I tell him what I've done, everything will be all dark and miserable just before I have to leave, and we've been so happy. Fergie said, "Don't you go nebbing around," and I did. But all the same it's no use — I've got to tell him before I go, somehow or other. Well, then, *why not now? Go on — get up and tell him now.*

She listened. And all at once, very faintly, she heard a door close and knew, from listening so often to the family's comings and goings on other nights, that it was the front door. In a flash she was out of bed and had pushed open her window. She leaned there with the wind pressing against her face and arms, billowing out the curtains, and saw his car down in the drive and saw him walking toward it.

"Uncle Dirk — *Uncle Dirk!*" But the wind had set up a great moaning and scurrying in the trees and swept her voice away. He got into the car and the motor started, the headlights sprang on in two long fingers of light, and in another moment the car swerved around and down the road among the trees.

It was nine-thirty when he drove off, and Cory built up her fire again in order to get warm. She lay there watching it, holding the carved box and planning how she would tell Uncle Dirk what she had done. Should she open the box? *Should she?* She put it down and leafed through the unicorn book, thinking and thinking and thinking, until at last, when it was almost eleven, she fell asleep.

Sixteen

FIVE hours later she awoke as sharply as if someone had spoken in her ear. But that someone was herself.

"I have got to open the box. And yet I can't because I'm already in Dutch deep enough as it is. Well, who knows whether it belongs to Uncle Dirk or not? But it does, I'll bet anything it does. I know it, and yet I have got to open it. And there's no proving it's his unless I *do* open it. Unless I wait until he gets home —"

She sat up and turned on the lamp, took the carved box in her lap and stared at it. Then she held it tightly in the crook of her arm while she tried to pull up the lid, but to no avail. She shook it, listening to the soft sliding inside. Nothing tinkled, so that it must be folded papers, she thought, or perhaps cloth. Why must she open it?

Now she got up and went to the dressing table and got a nail file she had seen in one of the drawers. Holding

the file tightly down near the tip, she pried and pried at
the lid on all sides, patiently, all the way around, until
gradually, very gradually, the lid began to be forced
very slightly upwards. Then she remembered that at
the very back of one of the drawers in the tall chest she
had seen a button hook with an ivory handle. She
found it, got into bed again, and once more held the
box firmly in the curve of her arm and, with the button

hook crooked under the barely raised lid, pulled up with all her might. Without warning the lid flew open, hitting her smartly and stingingly on the lips and spilling into her lap the entire contents of the box.

Wonderingly Cory picked up a white feather with a bright red tip that might have dropped from a woodpecker's wing, a dark purple feather with a greenish gloss, a brilliant yellowish-green one and another of brilliant blue. There were four shells wrapped in brittle Chinese paper: a reddish volcano keyhole limpet, a small blue chiton with pale green undersides, a large reddish-orange scallop and a most beautiful pearly monia. There was a paper that had been crushed and torn, then smoothed out again. And when Cory unfolded it, she read what was left of two verses about a quarrel and intense anger that were signed L.W.

There was a bracelet carved of some rich brown wood with the links interlocking and each cut so that there was a fine, upraised design on it. Finally, there was a silk scarf of deep lacquer red covered with a gray-green pattern. It was wrapped around a package of tissue paper, and inside the tissue was a chain with a silver unicorn on it. Cory had no need to compare to know that it was identical to her own. And when she turned it over there was the little rough place on the back as if it had been attached to something before being put on this chain. A tie pin, Uncle Dirk had said, down on the beach that first morning after she had come.

"I noticed your father had a silver unicorn tie pin and your mother had a unicorn on a chain around her neck. I'm glad you have hers."

"But the other one, Uncle Dirk? What happened to the other unicorn, the one on the tie pin?"

"Given away — or lost long ago, probably —"

Cory rubbed her finger back and forth across that rough place on the back of the unicorn where something had been attached. *Not lost* — not if this were it: her father's tie pin. *Not lost, because Laurel had had it.*

Cory stared at what had been in the box. *That is a woman's scarf, and a woman's bracelet, and Laurel wrote the poem. These are her things, put in this box that Uncle Dirk carved for her. And she had the unicorn that was my father's. So then — so then she must belong to me in some way. She must be part of my family, my mother's sister, or my father's. Oh, Laurel —!*

Cory knelt up in bed with the chain dangling from her hands, her whole being centered passionately upon the minute silver figure pressed between her hot palms. Then she sank back, for there could be some mistake, something she hadn't thought of. Yet why had she always felt about Laurel, from the very beginning, that she was someone special, from the moment her fingers had come down and found, as if by magic, Cory's unicorn buried in the sand?

By now Cory had a suffocating feeling in her chest, composed half of joy (for everything was right there, as plain as anyone could possibly make it) and half of fear that somewhere, somehow she had made some foolish mistake. Quickly she put everything back in the box and got up and went into the hall.

She must phone Laurel. She would speak very quietly down at the foot of the stairs, and as Uncle Dirk was gone and Grandmother was fast asleep, there would be no one to hear her ask, "Laurel, if we belong together — if we're related — surely you must have known. Why didn't you tell me? Why didn't *anyone* tell me?" There was the heart of the mystery: why had no one said anything? How could Laurel bear to know there was some connection between them and not have reached out her hand and said, "Cory, we are one family, you and I." I don't understand, thought Cory, going down the stairs. I just don't understand.

She turned on the lamp that stood near the phone, lifted up the telephone book, and leafed quickly through to find Laurel's number. Here it was. With her eyes still on it, so as not to forget and waste time, she dialed and waited. And then a voice, lightly enunciating with an artificial lilt, announced, *"This* — is a recording. You have reached a dis-connected number. Please be sure you are calling the right number and are dialing cor-rectly."

Cory went slowly back upstairs, hesitating outside Mrs. Van Heusen's room with her hand hovering above the knob. Softly she turned it, pushed open the door — and there lay Mrs. Van Heusen fast asleep, the little night light beside the bed revealing a worn, almost sad expression on her face as if she had gone to sleep with her head still paining her. She looked much, much older than when she was up and freshly dressed, and Cory knew that she couldn't possibly go over and wake her.

Back in her own room again, Cory sat down on the edge of the bed to think. There was only one thing to do. It was now half-past four, still dark, and she would have to go quickly, because Laurel's friends, she had said, were coming by for her at six-thirty to drive her to the Monterey airport. I will leave a note, Cory decided, just in case Uncle Dirk should come home and look in and find my bed empty.

Seventeen

CORY put on her jeans, a woolen shirt and her corduroy jacket. Then she wrote on a large piece of paper:

Dear Uncle Dirk — Don't worry about me. I have suddenly got an idea I have to talk about to Laurel. I went down in the store room and saw the masks of her and then I opened the carved box Peter and the others found down in the cave. She is going away in an hour or two and I have to see her before she leaves for *sure*. I'll be home about seven or eight, I guess. I know the way and will be careful.

Love —
Cory

This she left in the middle of the floor in the hall downstairs, with the lamp burning on the table. The carved box was under her arm. It was a quarter of five.

She had written, *Don't worry about me* — but when she opened the front door, she caught her breath in panic, for here was a world completely changed from what it had been last night. The wind had died long ago. The moon was gone. The stars were blotted out and in the just-paling dawn Cory saw that the whole coast was wrapped in fog — not thick, cotton-wool fog, but a ghostly, hovering mist that thinned to show dark shapes, then closed in again.

Such silence Cory had never known. Was the ocean still there? Yes, the fall of a wave came up hushed, and the wash of its retreat was a scarcely heard sigh. Cory stood looking and listening in an anguish of indecision. She had gone down to a room she had no business in; she had pried into a box that was not hers; and now she was setting out on a journey through the fog when it was still almost dark, so that it might be she would lose her way entirely. And if she ever *did* get to Laurel's, Laurel would probably be gone.

But all at once she closed the door behind her and set off around the house and through the rose garden toward the hedge. The tree shapes she knew so well loomed oddly in the dimness, distorted into strangers by the slow-moving mist. Yet now that she had made up her mind and was on her way, she was not really frightened any longer. She pressed into the hedge through the tunnel she had hollowed out for herself on previous trips, came out onto the hidden driveway, opened the honeysuckle-covered gate and went quickly on up and up to the top of the hill above Tarnhelm, where the cement foundation lay hidden in the drenched grass and where mysterious shapes of piled lumber were now half-seen, now hidden again. Then she ran all the way down the hill on the other side to the stone wall that bordered Tarnhelm acres.

Over the wall she went and out onto the highway. She knew that she must keep well away from the edge of it, that she must keep hidden by the undergrowth, because if she were seen by some passing motorist going in either direction, or by some early-morning hiker, she would be stopped and questioned and without doubt taken home.

Her fear had left her. Yes, at least just at first it had — as long as she was on Tarnhelm property. But now, as she left Tarnhelm woods behind and realized that she must recognize in the dimness and the fog that particular place on the other side of the highway where she and Peter left it to cross over the fields up past the Smallwoods' toward the forest, her heart sank again and the familiar hollow feeling began seeping into her stomach.

She ran across the road in order to be able to watch more closely for familiar signs. The dawn was becoming paler — becoming just perceptibly a translucent, pearly gray, so that if the mist had lifted at all, become even a shade thinner, Cory was sure she would be able

234

to recognize the path she must take. After a great many trees behind a long stretch of fence, there was only one mailbox and a road leading off the highway. Well, she had passed all that. Then you went on for a bit until you came to a huge big stump, another stretch of fence — and then there ought to be the path.

When Cory spied the stump, she felt like hugging it. And here was the last stretch of fence. The fog was thick at this point. She went peering along, her heart beating crazily as if it were jumping around any old way. But no, there couldn't possibly be any doubt. This *was* the path. And just as she turned in off the highway she heard her first car. Its headlights pierced the fog and Cory flattened, but she need not have bothered; the car roared on past, its driver looking neither left nor right.

She could have sung aloud as she started up across the meadow, for she could not go wrong now — not unless the fog came down all around her so that she could not even see her own feet. Yes, but the pearliness, the wavering translucence was lightening and spreading so that the shapes of trees were dark by comparison. They looked more like trees now than enormous, crouching robbers.

But one shape Cory couldn't be certain of. It appeared to move slightly. It looked like a cow — or perhaps a bull. This was the field with the bulls in it. The shape stood there, a little way off, and regarded her through the grayness, and now it did not move, nor did Cory. She went icy. If it started toward her and its big head should swing up, she would faint. She would simply not be there any more. Still, the shape did not move, and when Cory thought she could not endure this watchful, waiting stillness any longer, she knew suddenly that it was only the big rock she and Peter had climbed on a dozen times before they came to the Smallwoods' house and Toby came lunging out to welcome them.

Cory gave a ragged, gasping sigh, ran up to the rock and laid herself against it in blissful relief. Then, in an explosion —

"Yah-yah-yah-yah! R-r-r-r-r-*yah!* Yah-yah-yah!"

It was Toby, dingy and dim-sighted and bristling with fury, intent on defending the home place. But when he made out it was Cory, he lowered his heavy, sheepish head and pressed against her like a ton weight.

"Toby, you silly old thing," she said under her breath. "Be *still* —" and he slobbered on her hands, licking them, wagged his stub of a tail, and almost bent himself in two with delight — if a big, stout bulldog could ever be said to do such a thing — then trotted along quietly beside her, snuffling and blowing, and went back to his warm bed.

Now the black wall of the forest loomed up.

Out here in the fields it was almost light, almost full dawn. A meadow lark sent forth its first call — "*Sweeeeee-brocker-leeker-leeker.*" Silence. Then, again, "*Sweeeeee-brocker-leeker-leeker.*" But that was not it, nothing, nothing approaching the meadow lark's indescribably lovely call. Only it was the closest Cory could ever come to putting it into words, try as she had again and again, so that she could take it back with her to the New York apartment.

Just as she entered the deep gloom she had her first moment of thinking that she would have to turn back. Now she was frightened, thoroughly, coldly frightened. A faint, stealthy crackling came from the left, then ceased, and the silence that followed seemed far more tense, more alive, than any ordinary silence. Cory was shaking, but she made herself go on, quietly and steadily. She could barely make out the path which she and Peter, and just as often she alone, had taken many times. She knew what rocks to expect, what fallen trees, what rough banks with the stream whispering and trickling in its deep bed on the right, what rises and slight drops that all, gradually, led upward. When she crossed the rough little log bridge she felt comforted, her fears slightly allayed. It wasn't too much farther now. The going was steeper and she was warming again. She kept her head down, watching the path, climbing at a steady pace.

237

Then all at once came the shrill, warning cry of a gray squirrel that sounded through the forest with heart-stopping suddenness. Cory looked up.

On top of a rock ahead of her, not clearly to be made out because of the blurring light and the mist, she beheld a large cat shape. She could not tell if it was gray or pale brown, but it was a cat and it was very big. It was crouched in a humped position on the rock, its head toward her with its two ears standing up, its front paws together under its chin. It watched her fixedly, intently. Then its mouth opened and its lips lifted and it hissed, softly and slowly, "*H-h-h-h-h-h-h* — !"

Cory did not move. She remembered the skull Peter had found in the ravine. "I betcha it's a mountain lion's —" "But Andrew says they don't come this close to civilization, Peter. They stay way back in the hills —" "Anyhow, we found this skull right down there in the gorge —"

She never remembered afterward how long she and the mountain lion stared at each other. She was not aware of time passing; she stood in a timeless hollow of terror with every nerve stretched and alert for the cat's slightest shift. Then, suddenly, without seeming to move, it liquidly vanished from the rock. Cory caught a glimpse of its outstretched body, the long front legs reaching as it flashed to earth and made off down the mountain in the direction from which she had come.

Cory turned as if thinking of it circling in order to sneak up behind her. And without knowing what she was doing she began running, falling on the steep ascent, dropping the box, stumbling over it, snatching it up again, bruising and cutting her knees, but running, always running, and calling as she ran:

"*Laurel — Laurel — Laurel — !*"

Her pounding on the door seemed to echo through the whole forest, and when the door was snatched open, there was Laurel with her dressing gown half on and her hair streaming over her shoulders. Her eyes were wide and dark.

"*Cory — what in the name of heaven — ?*"

Cory was drawn in and the door banged behind her. The house was warm and softly lighted, and it smelled of coffee and toast and there was a fire burning on the hearth.

"Cory — what is it? — what is it? What's wrong — what's happened to you?"

With the box clasped to her chest, she looked up at Laurel, and abruptly she stopped "carrying on," as Fergie would have called it.

"Laurel," she said, "I saw a mountain lion."

Laurel gazed at her.

"But you couldn't have. They don't come down this far."

"All the same, I did. It was on a rock, and it looked

at me and hissed, and then after a long, long time it jumped off like lightning and streaked away through the trees — and I ran and ran and it was awful, because I was scared to death it might turn and follow me."

Laurel did not say anything for a second or two, and then she put her arm around Cory's shoulders and led her over to the couch and they sat down together.

"Was it sandy-colored or gray?"

"I'm not sure — I couldn't tell in that light —"

"Did it have round or pointed ears, and did it have a long tail or a stub?"

"Kind of pointed ears, and I didn't see its tail — or — yes, when it ran down the mountain — I think it was stubby."

"Then it was a bobcat, Cory — a lynx, or wildcat. *They* won't hurt you! But why are you here? Did you come to — ?" And then her eyes glanced down and she seemed to take in the box for the first time and, as if she could scarcely credit her senses, she took it and turned it over and over. "Why, where did you get it?" She stared up in wonderment, tried to open it, couldn't, and went on looking at Cory.

"Peter found it in the cave — the one on the side of the gorge, and I don't know who hid it there, but I'm sure it must be yours because I opened it —"

"Did your Uncle Dirk see it?"

"No. You see he's gone somewhere, Laurel. And

last night I went down into the big storeroom, the one you get to by going through his workroom and past the tower stairs. And I saw the chess set he made, and the furniture — everything I saw in my dream, but it *wasn't* a dream — it was real, and someone playing 'Greensleeves' was real. That's how I knew all at once, when I was looking at *The Lady and the Unicorn* in bed, and thinking about Smell and Sight and Taste and Touch and Sound. And I knew it was Uncle Dirk playing 'Greensleeves' very softly in the living room that night I was sick, because he's the only one who can play the piano besides Fergie, and she'd *never* go in and play without being asked, the way she was when Grandmother had her party. And so I went down into the storeroom, and there it all was, the chess set with the knights in the shape of unicorns and the dark king and queen who won't look at each other, and the happy, loving, light king and queen — and I found those masks Uncle Dirk carved of you. So then I knew you were the one he was going to marry and that maybe those were your poems all crushed up in the tower — *were* they?"

"Yes, Cory."

"And that was why Uncle Dirk was mad that Peter and I went snooping up there and found them. When I came back upstairs after being down in the storeroom, I heard Uncle Dirk out in the hall, and I was so scared

242

. . . I couldn't come out and tell him what I'd done, so I just stayed until he went in his room and I ran across and got into bed. Then he went away again and I fell asleep after a while, and when I woke up I knew I absolutely had to open the box. And I found the little silver unicorn on the chain and then I remembered what Uncle Dirk had told me, that my father had a tie pin with a unicorn on it — and, Laurel, when I turned your unicorn over, there was the little rough place on the back where the pin had been attached. So then I *knew* we were connected somehow, and I could hardly believe it. Oh but Laurel, if you had my father's tie pin, why didn't you tell me we belonged together? Are you my aunt, or *what* are you? You *must* be part of my family, but why wouldn't you tell me? Why wouldn't anybody tell me? How could you let me go away the other day without telling me?"

Laurel had sat there the whole time, with her eyes fixed on Cory's face while this great, long, breathless spate of words came pouring out. And her expression was such a strange, unreadable mixture of astonishment and uncertainty and — what else, what else? — that Cory simply could not make it out. Then Laurel reached over and took her hand in both her own.

"Because, Cory dear," and she looked as if she could hardly bear to say it, "because I'm not."

"Oh, but then I don't understand! I don't understand! Where did you get the little unicorn? Oh Laurel, I thought you'd *got* to be part of my family, my aunt, or *somebody* belonging to me —" and she flung herself down on the couch with both hands covering her face so Laurel couldn't see, because she could feel her chin crumpling up in the awful way she dreaded.

"Oh Cory, I'm sorry. I can't tell you how sorry. You see, it's really so simple. Your Uncle Dirk gave me the unicorn. Stephanie gave him your father's tie pin, and he had it put onto the chain for me."

"So then I *was* stupid, the way I thought I was being," sobbed Cory. "I knew I'd prob'ly made some absolutely ridiculous mistake —"

"But you didn't make a mistake," said Laurel gently. "Not exactly. You just didn't think about Uncle Dirk giving it to me. Cory, if I were really part of your family, do you think anything could have kept us apart for one moment? Nothing could have — *nothing!*"

Cory sat up, wiping the tears from her hot face.

"So that's why Uncle Dirk wouldn't answer when I asked him about the other unicorn. He just said it was prob'ly lost. He told me about the one I have, but he wouldn't really answer about yours. He wouldn't talk about you — and he *never* has, not once." Then, as she watched Laurel trying to open the box, "You have to have a nail file and a buttonhook. That's how I got it open."

Eighteen

FIVE minutes later the contents of the box lay in Laurel's lap.

"You see, Cory —" Then she glanced up at the clock. "Half an hour before my friends will come, and I'm all ready except for putting my dress on and doing up my hair. I packed my bags last night and the last-minute things this morning —"

"But about you and Uncle Dirk, Laurel?"

"I will tell you, but first let me make you a bowl of hot bread and milk." And when they were settled again, "It all began a long time ago when we were in high school —"

"— which was why you closed up the album," remembered Cory. "You were showing Peter and me those high-school pictures of you in *Romeo and Juliet*, and when I wanted to turn more pages, you said no, because you looked so thin. But it was really because you and Uncle Dirk were in there."

Yes, said Laurel. She had used to live in the house on the other side of Peter's, the side toward Carmel, above the beach, and they had known each other since they were children, she and Dirk. They'd explored together in the ravine, through the caves, hiked all over Point Lobos and the hills and up and down the coast. In those days, when they were both young, Dirk had been spoiled enough. But when Stephanie left for New York to make her own life, Mrs. Van Heusen's pride and indulgence all centered on him. Nothing was too good for him. He could have had anything in the world he wanted, and she never expected him to learn a profession and make a living. He was too gifted an artist for that, too fine a woodcarver.

"We became engaged in our last year at college, when we were at U.C. in Berkeley. And when we got home for our final summer vacation, Dirk decided not to finish college, and I asked him how he was going to earn a living. He just shrugged and said why should he earn a living when there was no need and he wanted only to carve? He was an artist and he intended to go on being one. If he managed to earn some money in his own way, in his own time, all well and good, but if not, what difference did it make?"

"But Laurel, didn't you *want* him to be an artist and carve?" demanded Cory.

"Of course I did, somehow or other! I would have

246

worked, or Dirk could have been an architect and combined the two. But I would not live on Mrs. Van Heusen's money and I didn't respect Dirk for being willing to. So we quarreled for the last time, and I've often wondered since if perhaps I was wrong, because it could have been that eventually he might have earned a living at what he really wanted to do.

"Anyway, I gathered up all these mementos of ours and took them over to Tarnhelm to give him, and I intended giving him back his ring as well. But when I got as far as the ravine, I happened to look up, and there he was on top of the cliff watching me. I called to him that I wanted to talk, and he stared back at me in silence for a moment or two, then turned away —"

"The dark king and queen," murmured Cory. "Or maybe the dark king and the light queen —"

"Yes. Dirk carved our moods into those pieces, didn't he, Cory? Anyway, I thought he was going to climb down," went on Laurel, "and that we would sit in our cave and talk and have a conference as we'd always done. And I waited and waited, but he never came, so then I knew we wouldn't see each other again. It was then I hid the box in the cave —"

"And your ring?" asked Cory. "What did you do with that? It isn't in the box."

"No," said Laurel, "because I threw it in the sea. I

was so enraged at the way Dirk had stood there look-ing down at me, cold and distant and hostile, that I just snatched it off, and I was filled with triumph, watching it circle through the air, flashing once as it fell. And I went back into the cave to get the box so that I could throw it in the water too, but I'd jammed it so tightly under a rock that I couldn't budge it. So I went back home and I finished college and Dirk didn't, and after a while my parents died and I sold that place and moved up here."

"How long ago was that?"

"Almost seven years ago."

Cory studied Laurel in silence.

"Why didn't you tell me before, Laurel?"

"If your Uncle Dirk had said anything to you about me, I would have."

"And *he* wouldn't, prob'ly thinking the same thing, because he could tell from the way I told him and Grandmother about you that you hadn't said anything. And maybe the whole time he was hoping and hoping you would. That's why, I bet, he never told me I shouldn't come up here." Laurel didn't answer. "Were *you* hoping he'd say something, Laurel?"

But Laurel only smiled and got up.

"Now I must go and dress," she said. "My friends will be here before I know it."

While Laurel was in the bedroom, Cory went into

the kitchen and washed Laurel's two or three breakfast dishes and the bread and milk bowl, and left everything tidy. And just as she was turning to go into the
other room, she heard a car drive up. "The friends,"
she said to herself, with a cold feeling inside. Now
everything was really finished. Then she heard feet running up the front steps, and there came a loud knocking at the door.

"Laurel! Laurel, it's Dirk —" There was not a single
sound, as if the house had suddenly drawn in upon
itself and stopped breathing. Cory saw Laurel standing
at her bedroom door with her dress on and her hands
up to her head putting in a hairpin. *"Laurel — is Cory
with you?"*

As if she were moving in her sleep, Laurel went over
to the door and opened it, and Uncle Dirk stared first
at her, a long, long look, and then over at Cory. He
came in, and Laurel closed the door behind him.

"I woke up and went into the hall," he said to Cory,
"and saw the light from your room. And when I read
your note and saw the fog outside, I didn't see how
you could possibly get up here alone." Again he turned
and looked at Laurel — as if he couldn't look at her
enough, thought Cory.

"She saw a bobcat," said Laurel in a strange, stiff
voice. "Poor child, she was terrified. She thought it
was a mountain lion."

249

"But mountain lions don't come down to the coast," said Uncle Dirk as if thinking of something else and still with his eyes fixed on Laurel's face. Then he took his gaze away and looked at Cory again. "Why didn't you just wake me up? What got into your head to come up here alone?"

"But I didn't know you had come back, Uncle Dirk. I saw you go — and then you must have come back while I was asleep. You see, I went downstairs — I mean I went down into the big storeroom and saw all the things I'd thought were in my dream, only that part wasn't a dream because, the time I was sick, I was actually wandering around in a fever trying to get a drink of water. And last night when I went down, I found the masks of Laurel, and then when I came up again you were out in the hall." Now Cory's heart was thudding the way it had done when she'd stood in the workroom listening to him sing the song about the man named Oh, By Jingo, but she went stubbornly ahead and told him the rest of the story.

And while she was telling him this, Laurel came over and stood near him. And when Cory was finished, Uncle Dirk began looking around as if he wanted to take in every detail he'd tried to picture all these years — the house Laurel lived in, the view she had, the chairs she would sit in, the shape of the rooms. Then he looked down at Laurel, and suddenly their arms came out, Laurel's and Uncle Dirk's, both at once, and they came together and held each other close.

"Oh, Laurel!" said Uncle Dirk. "Laurel — Laurel, I've wanted to come up here so many times — *so many times* —" After that, nobody said anything, and then, after a while, they stood apart again, but with their hands still closed about each other's. "Cory, there's something I've got to ask Laurel. Would you go out and sit in the car for about five minutes? Then I'll drive you home and Laurel can get unpacked, because I don't think she's going anywhere. Not just yet, at any rate."

Cory never, as long as she lived, forgot any least part of that drive back to Tarnhelm.

"Why, Cory," cried Fergie when she and Andrew, back from San Francisco, came into the kitchen that afternoon, "ye're a' lichted up. Ye look positively incandescent! What's happened, child?"

Incandescent. Yes, thought Cory many times afterward, that was ex-*actly* the way she had felt, shining, glowing, blooming with light. It began on the way back, when even the coast became incandescent as she and Uncle Dirk drove along, down the mountain and out onto the highway. The sun was beginning to

break through, and as its light gradually warmed, the mists became pale golden, a gold that slowly deepened until the whole countryside was set coolly afire.

Uncle Dirk came out of Laurel's house and silently got into the car. And as they drove away, Cory hardly dared to look at him, or to speak. But when she stole a glance sideways, she saw him glance at her in the same instant, and his eyes were kindling.

"Uncle Dirk — she said *yes!*"

He did not reply for a second, and then he let out a great burst of laughter, almost a shout of joy.

"She said *yes!* She said *yes!* Oh, she said yes, all right, Cory. But do you know what? She said, 'I'll marry you, Dirk. Of course I'll marry you, on one condition. And that's that we adopt Cory, if Stephanie will let us.'"

That was the thunderbolt, Cory told Fergie and Andrew afterwards. *That* was the moment of incandescence. She could not believe what she was hearing, and when she turned to look at Uncle Dirk, she was scarcely able to get out the words.

"And — and — *are* you?"

"*Are* we! Well, of course. You want to be Laurel's child, and she wants you, and I already feel as if you're mine. So why shouldn't you be? Stephanie's never adopted you — no doubt knowing, all this time, that her life isn't fitted at all to bringing up a child."

"Uncle Dirk, do you suppose she'll let me be yours and Laurel's?"

"I haven't the slightest doubt she will. In fact, I think she'll be overjoyed. I think it's probably troubled her all these years that she's not been giving you the kind of home life you'd like to have, or ought to have, what with those confounded lady-helps and one thing and another."

"I don't know about that," said Cory. "I don't think she's ever thought about it, really. And I think she's looking forward like the dickens to having this house in the country."

"Well, don't worry. We'll fix things, Cory, so just don't worry."

"And so I'm not worrying," said Cory blissfully to

Fergie and Andrew. "I refuse to worry. I'm going to be happy. Uncle Dirk's been up at Laurel's all day, and they're making plans."

"Oh, my, how I hope it wur-r-rks!" exclaimed Fergie, looking as if she'd been listening to a story of Cory's flight to the moon or some such other incredible experience. "I *do* hope it wur-r-rks — ye couldn't bear to be disappointed now —"

"Well, why on ear-rth *should* there be any disappointment, I'd like to know?" demanded Andrew, his bronze eyes widening and his eyebrows going up with indignation the way they always did under such circumstances. "Why *should* there be disappointment? I can't imagine Miss Stephanie being anything but delighted for Cory's sake."

"How did Mrs. Van take it?" Fergie wanted to know next.

Cory leaned back in her chair and smiled at them, beatific — in other words, serene and joyous.

"Grandmother still wasn't up yet when Uncle Dirk left me here and went back up to Laurel's. But when I got to her door, she must have heard me because she called out — and I went in. And just like you, Fergie, the minute she saw me she knew something absolutely tre-*men*dous must have happened. And when I announced it, 'Grandmother, Uncle Dirk and Laurel are going to get married, and they're going to adopt me,' she stared at me as if I'd gone right out of my head, and she put her hand across her eyes. Then she took it down and I could see she was happy, and she wanted to know exactly how it had all happened, and then she said, 'Oh Cory, you *are* bewitched after all, aren't you? In the best possible way. You weren't born cawry-fisted for nothing. Come here and let me hug you.' And so I did, and she was just as happy as she could possibly be because she's always been so fond of Laurel, though she's only seen her once in a great while downtown. And I sat there cross-legged at the foot of the bed and we talked and talked about everything, and then I came down here and got breakfast for both of us and took it up on a tray, and we sat there and ate together and it was just like, for the first time — no, the second time — she was really my grandmother. And then after that she got up and dressed because she had to go to a luncheon and a club meeting, and that's where she is now."

As Cory finished speaking, Andrew all at once reached out and drew an air-mail envelope with Japanese stamps on it from the pile of letters and magazines and circulars that he and Fergie had brought up from the mailbox.

"For you, I believe, Cory —" and he handed it to her.

256

It was from Stephanie, and it said that she would arrive on the twelfth, which would be the next day, on the two o'clock plane, and would somebody please come to the Monterey airport to meet her.

"Ah," said Fergie, "it won't be long now, will it, darling?"

Nineteen

STEPHANIE talked constantly from the moment she was led to the car until they arrived at Tarnhelm. It was as if she were warding off any words of Cory's, as if she wanted no questions asked, and so put up a wall of words of her own about her tour and about Japan and her friends there as if she were giving a travel lecture full of such dramatic and spilling-over excitement that Cory wondered what Andrew could possibly be thinking.

Now Cory and Uncle Dirk and Grandmother and Stephanie were all in the living room together, with Stephanie standing at the fireplace and the others sitting around watching her as if they were an audience. She looked perfect, Cory decided.

She had on a white silk blouse and a bottle-green suit she had had made in Hong Kong, and her now red-gold hair (blond when she had left New York) was as smooth and shining as it was possible for it to be and beautifully shaped to her head. I'll never look like that, Cory told herself, never. But maybe I could look a little like Laurel. Ye could look like yerself, she heard Fergie say, as clearly as if the words had been spoken aloud, and I think that by the time ye're sixteen or seventeen, that will be quite satisfactory.

"Oh Cory, what a time we'll have, you and I," Stephanie was saying, "going through our rooms, one by one, and planning colors and just what furniture we'll need. I can't wait to get back! Don't you feel that way?" Then her face changed suddenly; all the light went out of it and she studied Cory. "Well, what on earth is the matter with you? You've been as solemn as an owl ever since I got off the plane. Oh, it's *that* — the business you wrote about."

"She's waited a long time, Stephanie," reminded Mrs. Van Heusen.

"Yes, but it does seem as if I might be let to enjoy myself for half an hour at least. Very well, then — here goes." She tossed herself down in the wing chair near the fireplace where Mrs. Van Heusen always sat in the evenings when Cory and Uncle Dirk played chess. There she looked smaller, somehow, suddenly unhappy. "You must understand I've never really known what to do about you. I've just done the best I could and it's been hard sometimes, but I've always realized I wasn't managing very well —"

"But why did you take me at *all*, Stephanie?"

"Because your mother was my dearest friend and I would have done anything for her. And if it hadn't been for me, she and your father would never have gone to Switzerland. I asked them to come —"

"Oh, but Stephanie," said Mrs. Van Heusen, "they made up their own minds. You can't take the blame for that —"

"But at the time I did. I did! And when your mother asked me to keep you, Cory, I said I would, even though I had misgivings. Both your father's parents were dead, and there was only Coralie's mother, but Coralie wanted me to have you because her mother was quite old and not at all the kind of person to care for a small child. And there's an aunt of yours in England, but she has a great brood of children and not very much money. So I promised Coralie I would keep you and do everything I could for you — and I *have* kept you ever since."

Cory gazed at Stephanie in silence, turning it all over in her mind. Then, after a little —

"Why haven't you ever told me?"

"Because there was never any time," returned Stephanie impatiently, almost angrily. "Never the *right* time, somehow." She got up and began walking up and down the way she always did when she was restless and nervous. "You know the kind of life I have, Cory — there's always something. And the reason I've never adopted you is because I kept hoping — that is, I mean," she stumbled, and her face flushed, "I kept thinking that perhaps somebody in your family I'd never heard of might come forward and say they would like to take you — somebody who would be better suited than I — and yet, it *hasn't* been too bad, after all, has it, Cory?" Stephanie turned and smiled all at once, one of her dazzling smiles.

"No-o," said Cory slowly. "And it's always nice when you get home — at least at first. It's just the moving all the time, and never really getting to make friends, and then the lady-helps —"

"But don't you see, we're not going to have that any more. Oh, I've been thinking about nothing else! We're going to have a real home and get a good house-keeper, somebody who'll be just right. And I *will* adopt you — I promise —"

"But Stephanie," said Cory, and it was her turn to smile, "you don't have to. Not now. Because we've got it all planned — Laurel and Uncle Dirk are going to get married and they want to adopt me and you won't have to bother any more about lady-helps, and you won't have to move to the country when really you couldn't stand it. Because it isn't the country that matters. Now I'm going to have a real father and mother, and we'll stay that way and live in one place and I'll go to one school and everything will be much better and easier for you."

Cory was by this time sitting right out on the edge of her chair with her hands clasped between her knees, and she never realized until afterwards how tightly she had her fingers gripped together. But curiously enough, Stephanie was staring all around at everyone, then especially at Cory, and slowly her face changed.

"You can't mean it," she said softly. "You can't mean that after all these years of our being together, you've been planning secretly all to yourself to just say 'Thanks!' and desert me."

Cory's astonishment was so complete that she couldn't get out a single word. But Mrs. Van Heusen could. And she must have been enormously angry because her eyes shot sparks.

"Ri-*dic*ulous, Stephanie! I have never in all my life heard anything so ridiculous. You just got through confessing how you've never known what to do about Cory and how hard it's been for you, and now you —"

"Of course it's been hard," exclaimed Stephanie, going into her deep, carrying stage voice, the one edged all purple with loneliness and bravery. "Of *course* it has." She got up and went over to the windows and stood there facing them. "But I've got enough money at last and it's not going to be hard any more, and I thought we could have a real home together. I can't *tell* you how I've been looking forward to it — and now what good will it be without Cory?"

"But it isn't the *house* that matters, Stephanie," burst out Cory desperately, almost in tears. "It isn't that. You don't understand —" and she got up and ran into the hall, her disappointment too terrible to be shown in front of everyone. Fergie and Andrew were in the kitchen, and she closed the door and flung herself down at the table with her head in her arms. But the voices still reached them, for it turned out that all the Van Heusens, when excited, had carrying tones.

"You know perfectly well you've always hated the country —" came Uncle Dirk's voice, blazing with indignation.

"I have not — and I *will* have my house and my trees and fields and horses and stables and everything just as I've planned, and I *will* not give up Cory —"

On and on it went, but at last it quieted and Cory got up and went down the hall to the living room and there was Stephanie crying — not sniffing and hiccoughing messily into a handkerchief, with her nose and eyes all blurry and red, but looking quietly straight ahead across the room with tears rolling down her face. And even though Cory suspected they might be stage tears, she felt sick.

"Stephanie," she said, "I didn't understand. I'll go back to New York with you. And it's not true I don't care about you — I heard you say that. Only I *did* want to stay here, and I thought you'd like it that way."

But strange, unpredictable Stephanie! She stared at Cory for a moment, and then:

"Oh, no — indeed you will not go back to New York with me. I wouldn't dream of taking you back as long as you prefer not to come."

And she walked past them all without once looking up and went out of the room.

Twenty

THE FOLLOWING morning, which was Saturday, clouds the size of ten castles in one were being bowled across the sky by a great blustering, flurrying wind. It sang around the corners of Tarnhelm, the gulls were swept helter-skelter and even blown backwards at times, and the low-flying cormorants, trying to travel in neat V's as usual, about a foot above the waves, were tossed every which way without dignity. The whole ocean was being whipped into little separate, hurrying crests of foam.

Cory, her jacket buttoned up under her chin and her hands dug deep into her pockets, butted into a wall of wind and bored her way across the grass toward the shortcut. There'd been a phone call right after breakfast.

"Hi," said Peter. "This is me. Could you come on

over and bring that box? Did you get it open? *Is* it your uncle's?"

"No," said Cory, "it isn't. And I can't bring it because Laurel's got it. It's hers."

"Laurel W*oodford's?* Well, how — ?"

"I'll tell you when I see you —"

"O.K.," said Peter. "Come to the cave right away — the little one up on the path. Say, why do you sound so funny? Has something happened?"

"Yes," said Cory, "a whole lot's happened," and she hung up before Peter could ask anything else.

At the sea wall she stood for a second looking out over the Pacific while she caught her breath, but at once heard a far-off swept-about shouting, and turned and there was Peter near the little dug-out place waving his arms.

They curled themselves inside with their knees drawn up, and Cory thought how this was just like the first time, only now it was wind driving across the entrance instead of rain. Then she began telling, and Peter's green eyes grew wide, especially when she came to the part about the bobcat she'd thought was a mountain lion. But he didn't bother making fun of her when later in the story she had to admit she'd been mistaken. He listened with his whole self, sunk over his ears in suspense. And when she told how Uncle Dirk had asked Laurel to marry him — again, after

266

all these years — and she'd said yes, if they could adopt Cory, his eyes grew even bigger.

"*Adopt* you! Honest? You mean it? But I thought —"

"I know, Peter, so did I — but Stephanie never had adopted me, because of reasons —"

"So then you're going to stay. You're going to live here —"

"But then Stephanie came," went on Cory, and found now that she couldn't tell even Peter all that had been said, only that Stephanie wanted to buy a big house and was determined that Cory should go back with her. "I almost couldn't bear it, but when I finally told her that I *would* go back with her, why then — she just looked at me and said that she wouldn't dream of taking me when I didn't really want to go."

What a terrible time that had been. Cory could remember Fergie's exact words: "I told Mrs. Van it's as if a spell has been cast over all our happiness."

"But how strange, Fergie. That's exactly what I thought a long time ago when I couldn't find Van Heusen in the telephone book and I thought maybe Mrs. Smallwood was a witch. But of course I was just making up."

"Well, yer granny says the spell that's been cast is the one you put on Mr. Dirk and Miss Laurel —"

"But a good one, Fergie?"

"Aye, a *good* one, darling!"

Yet now everything was blighted. Laurel even said, when Uncle Dirk phoned her, that she did not see how they could go ahead, and dinner had been almost silent last night because Stephanie had gone out of the house late in the afternoon without saying a word to anyone and had not returned.

Now Cory lifted her eyes and looked at Peter, coming back out of remembering.

"When I was almost asleep, after I'd gone to bed, I heard feet running up the stairs, and I couldn't believe it was Stephanie, coming up that fast. But it was, and she opened the door and came in and sat on my bed in the dark and didn't say anything and *didn't* say anything, and I just looked up at her and waited — and finally —"

Cory was certain that that moment would stay inside of her for the rest of her life, no matter how long she lived.

"I'm so ashamed, Cory. I didn't mean all I said. You know how I am — I've done this before. If you were to ask me what happens when I get like that, closed up and — refusing to see — I wouldn't be able to tell you. All the time I'm going on making everybody wretched and myself the most wretched of all, I know I'm wrong and I can't seem to admit it. But I'm sorry, Cory. And I want you and Laurel and Dirk to stay together — I could hardly wait to get home and tell you that. It was my hurt vanity that got in the way, that you'd chosen them instead of me and that you'd all gone ahead and planned everything without my knowing." She leaned over and kissed Cory and they held each other tightly for a moment. "I'll be leaving early tomorrow morning and you won't be awake. So I'll say goodbye now."

"Goodbye, Stephanie —" Their hands came together, and then Stephanie got up and went to the door, and it closed behind her.

"Well, why *did* she come up?" demanded Peter, indignant at being left in mid-air. "Why *did* she?"

"To tell me she wanted me to stay, and that she'd been hurt, but all the same she wanted me to be with Laurel and Uncle Dirk and be their daughter. And now Uncle Dirk says we'll live on the mountain at Laurel's while we plan the new house where it was always going to be —"

"Up there where the foundation is?"

"Yes, up there above Tarnhelm. And I'm going to go to your school, Peter, and stay here forever and ever and I'm *never* going to go away."

Peter sat quiet, thinking.

"And it was because of me, kind of, wasn't it?" he said presently. "I mean, if I hadn't found the box —"

"I know. Oh Peter, I can hardly believe it."

"But remember what Andrew said. You're cawry-fisted —"

At that moment, just as the wind died for a bit, they heard shouting coming up from below, and at once Peter was out of the cave.

"We're co-ming!" he called, and he turned as Cory

scrambled after him. "It's the Explorers. We were going to have a farewell party, and that's why I asked you to come over, but now it'll be an initiation instead. *Wait'll* they hear!"

Away he went, tearing along the cliff with Cory after him, her arms spread wide as if, like the gulls over her head, she was sailing on the wind.